John F. Kennedy
35th President of the United States

Lucille Falkof

GARRETT EDUCATIONAL CORPORATION

Cover: *Official photographic portrait of John F. Kennedy.*
(Copyright Bachrach Inc.)

Copyright © 1988 by Lucille Falkof

All rights reserved including the right of reproduction in whole or in part in any form without the prior written permission of the publisher. Published by Garrett Educational Corporation, 130 East 13th Street, P.O. Box 1588, Ada, Oklahoma 74820.

Manufactured in the United States of America

Edited and produced by Synthegraphics Corporation

Library of Congress Cataloging in Publication Data

Falkof, Lucille, 1924–
 John F. Kennedy, 35th President of the United States.

 (Presidents of the United States)
 Bibliography: p.
 Includes index.
 Summary: Presents the childhood, education, employment, and political career of the youngest man ever elected president of the United States.
  1. Kennedy, John F. (John Fitzgerald), 1917–1963 – Juvenile literature. 2. Presidents – United States – Biography – Juvenile literature. 3. United States – Politics and government – 1961–1963 – Juvenile literature. [1. Kennedy, John F. (John Fitzgerald), 1917–1963. 2. Presidents] I. Title.
 II. Title: John F. Kennedy, thirty-fifth president of the United States. III. Series.
 E842.Z9F35 1988 973.922'092'4 [B] [92] 87-35954
 ISBN 0-944483-03-8

John F. Kennedy
35th President of the United States

Contents

Chronology for John F. Kennedy ... vii

Chapter 1: Beyond the Call of Duty ... 1

Chapter 2: Born into Politics ... 13

Chapter 3: The Education of a Kennedy ... 21

Chapter 4: Following the Family Tradition ... 29

Chapter 5: The Senator Takes a Wife and a Gamble ... 43

Chapter 6: The Campaign Trail: Winning the Nomination ... 53

Chapter 7: The Youngest President ... 67

Chapter 8: The White House, Kennedy Style ... 79

Chapter 9: The Heights and the Depths ... 89

Chapter 10: Standing Firm ... 95

Chapter 11: "Promises to Keep" ... 107

Bibliography ... 113

Index ... 117

Chronology for John F. Kennedy

1917 Born on May 29 in Brookline, Massachusetts

1931–1934 Attended Choate, a private school in Wallingford, Connecticut

1936–1940 Attended Harvard University, graduated *magna cum laude*

1941–1945 Served as naval lieutenant in World War II; survived crash of PT boat 109 in August 1943

1947–1952 Served as Democratic congressman from the 11th Congressional District, Boston, Massachusetts

1953–1960 Served as Democratic senator from Massachusetts

1953 Married Jacqueline Lee Bouvier on September 12 in Newport, Rhode Island

1957 Won Pulitzer Prize for biography for his book, *Profiles in Courage*

1961 Inaugurated January 20 as 35th President of the United States; Bay of Pigs disaster, April 17–19

1962 Cuban missile crisis, October 16–28

1963 "*Ich bin ein Berliner*" speech at Berlin Wall in June; Nuclear Test Ban Treaty concluded, July 25; assassinated in Dallas, Texas, November 22

Official presidential portrait of John F. Kennedy by Aaron Shikler.
(Copyrighted by the White House Historical Association;
photograph by the National Geographic Society.)

Chapter 1
Beyond the Call of Duty

There was no doubt that there was going to be trouble on the night of August 1, 1943. The squadron of American PT (patrol-torpedo) boats was stretched across a passage between two small South Pacific islands, waiting to intercept some expected Japanese supply ships. In the grand pattern of World War II, this was only a minor skirmish in the great Pacific war.

Operating on a single engine to reduce its noise level, PT 109 idled quietly back and forth in the water. Wearing their life jackets, the crew peered through the darkness of the moonless night. On the bridge, the boat's commander, Lt.,J.G., John F. Kennedy, and Ensign George Ross maintained their vigil.

Both men saw the shape at the same time. They watched for a moment as it drew nearer. Suddenly they realized it was not another PT boat. As Kennedy shouted an alarm, the Japanese destroyer shifted course, positioning itself to ram the American boat. PT 109, operating on only the one engine, coud not maneuver quickly enough. The steel prow of the destroyer sliced through the boat, cutting it in half.

IN SEARCH OF BATTLE

Jack Kennedy did not have to be there. In fact, he had to fight his way into the armed forces and then into combat. After graduation from college and six months of graduate school, he had tried to enlist. He failed to pass the physical examination for both the Army's Officer Candidate School and the Navy.

Kennedy was one of eight children of one of the richest families in America. But he was raised to be competitive, to offer service to his country, and to respect bravery. He left school and, in the summer of 1940, returned to the family home in Hyannis Port, Massachusetts, to undergo a strenuous exercise program. It worked. In September he passed his physical exam and was inducted into the Navy.

His first assignment was in the Office of Naval Intelligence in Washington, D.C. When the Japanese attacked Pearl Harbor, Hawaii, on December 7, 1941, Jack wanted to leave his desk job and go to sea. But it wasn't until the following July that he received assignment to Midshipmen's School at Northwestern University, outside of Chicago.

At the school, students were asked to volunteer for duty on PT boats. Jack Kennedy's hand shot up. Junior officers who served on the small boats received a command much more rapidly than those who had to work their way up on the large ships.

Jack had a large amount of sailing experience because his family had always owned boats and sailed in the Atlantic waters off their Cape Cod home. So it wasn't surprising that he received top grades in both engineering and ship handling. In fact, he did too well. When his classmates left for sea duty, Jack was kept on as an instructor. Only the application of some influence by his father, who was the American ambassador to England, freed him for combat assignment.

In the Combat Zone

If action was what Jack Kennedy wanted, the Solomon Islands was the right place to be. The island of Tulagi, where he was first stationed, had been captured by the Japanese five months after Pearl Harbor. During the invasion of Guadalcanal by U.S. forces in August 1942, the Americans also recaptured Tulagi.

Kennedy's arrival in the Solomons was marked by a Japanese bombardment of Guadalcanal. The night before his landing, as his ship was steaming toward Tulagi, the Japanese launched an air attack on the area. Bombs landed so close to Jack's ship that water splashed onto the decks. He watched in horror as an American destroyer was ripped apart by bombs from a Japanese fighter plane.

Within two weeks, Jack assumed command of his own boat—PT 109. It was only nine months old, but already it was scarred by bullets and shells from its engagements with the enemy. It was also grimy and infested with rats and cockroaches.

More important, the crew assigned to Lt. Kennedy was "green," mostly men as inexperienced in combat as he was. The only crew member who had served on the boat previously was Ensign Leonard Thom, a huge blond, bearded man who looked like a warrior on an ancient Viking ship. He became the executive officer, Kennedy's right-hand man.

PT 109 had to be scraped, cleaned, sanded, and painted. Lt. Kennedy worked right alongside his men. The crew came to admire and respect the new captain. They also enjoyed his relaxed attitude toward Navy regulations. He often walked around stripped to the waist, wearing sunglasses and a variety of headgear ranging from Marine fatigue caps to baseball caps to a yachting hat with a visor one-foot long.

A picture of Jack Kennedy taken while on duty with the United States Navy in the Solomon Islands during World War II. (John F. Kennedy Library.)

Dangerous Waters

The first few months after the boat was repaired were spent on routine patrols. Life seemed pretty monotonous. Emphasizing that feeling was the food, which was limited in variety and consisted mostly of canned meat, canned sausages, and baked beans. The crew admired Kennedy's ingenuity in finding a continuous supply of powdered ice cream. Their captain had a real "sweet tooth." He loved pancakes and candy. Occasionally, he would come up with a dozen eggs, a loaf of fresh bread, and, best of all, a package of 24 candy bars.

In mid-July 1943, PT 109 was ordered to Rendova, one of a group of islands called New Georgia. American and allied forces in the Pacific were preparing an offensive against another island in the chain, on which the Japanese had built a vital airstrip. The Japanese, anticipating the attack, were shipping supplies and reinforcements to the base. In the blackness of night, Japanese destroyers and motorized barges would sneak among the islands, ferrying supplies. PT boats from Rendova were assigned to intercept these ships.

On the very first night after its arrival at Rendova, PT 109 was sent out on patrol. The islands and the passages between the islands were just so many lines on a map that first time out. But after several nightly patrols around the islands, the lines on the map became real, matching the outlines seen through the darkness of night.

At Rendova, the war was real, too. The flashes and lights from shore batteries, the swoosh of shells before they dropped nearby, and the rumors and talk about casualties began to affect the crew. The men started to talk about how they would act if attacked. Would they be afraid? Would they allow themselves to be captured? Would they fight to the death?

The patrols were conducted in blackness: black sky, black waters, black shadows and shapes. Sometimes the gun-

The crew of PT boat 109 before it was destroyed in August 1943. On the right, in dark glasses, is the skipper, Jack Kennedy. (John F. Kennedy Library.)

ners were ordered to shoot, but in the blackness it was hard to know if the target was another PT boat or an enemy ship.

The Sinking of PT 109

There was no doubt that the night of August 1, 1943, was going to be filled with trouble. A coded message, warning of a Japanese supply run, had barely been received when Japanese bombers tore out of the sky, dropping their bombs on the boats sitting in the harbor. By the time the attack was over, two PT boats had been sunk and a third damaged.

At 6:30 P.M., as the equatorial sun dipped below the horizon, 15 PT boats snaked out of Rendova Harbor. Positioned in a passage called Blackett Strait, the men of PT 109, wearing their life jackets, peered through the moonless sky looking for Japanese supply ships. Operating on a single engine to keep the noise level down, the PT boat moved quietly back and forth in the water.

On the deck of PT 109, Lt. Kennedy was at the wheel. Near him stood Ensign George Ross, a friend whose own boat had been sunk and who had volunteered to go out with Kennedy that night. It was past midnight when suddenly a Japanese destroyer loomed out of the darkness. Both men saw the Japanese ship at the same time, just as it shifted course and headed straight toward the small PT boat. But the PT boat was moving too slowly to be able to take any evasive action. Kennedy barely had time to shout an alarm to his crew when the steel prow of the Japanese destroyer rammed into PT 109, cutting it in half.

ISLAND HOPPING TO SURVIVAL

The impact of the crash with the Japanese destroyer slammed Kennedy's back against a steel reinforcing brace. Fire burst from the gasoline tanks below the deck.

The bow of the boat, where he had been standing, was still afloat. Kennedy called out, asking for survivors to identify themselves. Two men were missing. Kennedy dove overboard to find them, but their bodies never were found. Among the survivors, two had been seriously injured. One of them, Patrick McMahon, had been caught in the engine room and was badly burned.

The men clung to the floating hulk for the remainder of the night, hoping that daylight would bring rescue. But when morning came, they recognized the larger islands surrounding them and knew they were held by the Japanese. By afternoon, Kennedy realized that headquarters probably counted the crew as dead. They were lucky not to have been spotted by the Japanese; but if they continued to sit in the passage, they would soon be seen by the enemy.

They decided to swim to an island, called Plum Pudding, three miles away. A plank from the boat helped the others to swim, but McMahon was too badly burned to make it on his own. Taking a strap from McMahon's life jacket between his teeth, Kennedy positioned the injured man, back to back, behind him and started to swim. It took Kennedy almost four hours to tow McMahon to the island. The pain in his back did not help. By the time they reached the island, the two men had only enough strength to crawl ashore.

A Change for the Better

Kennedy and his officers checked their supplies—a .38 caliber revolver, three knives, a battle lantern, and a flashlight—and discussed their situation. Their only hope, they decided, was to attract the attention of PT boats patrolling the nearby passage.

That night, August 2, Kennedy swam to the center of the passage, towing the lantern and his life jacket. For hours he treaded water, but no boats came. Wearily, he swam back to his men. The next night, Ensign Ross made the swim, but he had no better results.

On August 4, Kennedy decided they should move closer to the passage. The island of Olasana was a suitable location; it also appeared to have a more abundant supply of coconuts. So, once more the 11 survivors struggled into the water and swam to their next refuge. Again, Kennedy towed the injured McMahon.

Now Kennedy and Ross turned their eyes on a small island, Nauru, that sat in the middle of the passage. Although they thought the Japanese might have a lookout on the island, the two men decided to explore this new position.

Eyes of the Natives

The PT 109 crew was unaware that they already had been spotted. Two island natives, Biuku Gasa and Eroni Kumana, had reported the survivors' whereabouts to an Australian coastwatcher.

Lt. Arthur Reginald Evans held one of the most dangerous of all military jobs. Coastwatchers were hidden, often on enemy-held islands, in places where they could observe movements of men and shipping. They reported their sightings by radio. Coastwatchers also relied on loyal natives to supply information. Evans was situated on the very island the allies were planning to invade when his native informants told him about the PT boat and its missing crew.

On Nauru, Kennedy and Ross crossed paths with Evans' information gatherers. As Kennedy and Ross were inspecting the wreckage of a small Japanese boat, the two natives saw the Americans less than a mile away. At a distance, it was difficult to identify who the men were—they might have been Japanese soldiers. Biuku and Eroni didn't wait to find out. They raced for their dugout canoe and paddled furiously—to Olasana.

There they were spotted by the nine other survivors. Ensign Thom tried to rush up to them. But the sight of the bearded, blond giant startled the natives so much they began back-paddling their canoe. Thom ran to the water's edge shouting, "Navy, Navy, American, American." Now, at a safe distance, the two natives stopped and listened.

"White star!" shouted Thom and pointed to the sky. The natives understood. The white star was the insignia on American aircraft. The natives had been told to help airmen who crashed or parachuted from planes with the white star.

Welcome Messages

The next morning, August 6, Lt. Kennedy returned to Olasana, where he immediately established communications with the two natives. Using sign language and repeating the name "Rendova" again and again, he managed to explain to Biuku and Eroni that he wanted them to carry a message to Naval headquarters. Using a quarter of a coconut as "paper" and his knife as "pen," he scratched out a message:

NAURO ISL   NATIVE KNOWS POSIT
HE CAN PILOT   11 ALIVE   NEED
SMALL BOAT
KENNEDY

Thom also scribbled a message with a pencil stub and a piece of paper he found in his pocket. The two messages were entrusted to Biuku and Eroni, who then began paddling the 38 miles to Rendova.

The natives stopped at an island where an English-speaking scout radioed the messages to Evans, who had since moved to Gomu Island, away from the Japanese airfield. He immediately sent seven native scouts by canoe to Olasana. They carried with them a letter from Evans and also some supplies.

The Rescue

The arrival of the native scouts was hailed with utter joy. Kennedy and his men were grimy, starving, and half naked. The feast spread before them seemed sent from heaven—yams, potatoes, rice, boiled fish, and canned roast beef hash. The natives scrambled to bring down coconuts from the trees, and the meal was served in dishes made from coconut shells and with spoons made from palm fronds.

After the meal, Kennedy was hidden in the bottom of the canoe and ferried to Gomu. As he came ashore, Evans greeted him and, in his clipped Australian accent, said, "Come and have some tea." Over tea they planned the rescue.

Evans radioed headquarters to pick up Lt. Kennedy at a nearby point. At 10 P.M., a PT boat slipped up to a canoe where Kennedy was waiting in the dark. Someone called out, "We've got some food for you." Came the reply: "No, thanks. I've just had a coconut."

It was after midnight when the PT boat, with Kennedy aboard, reached Olasana. At the first shouts from Kennedy, the men raced—or hobbled—to the shore. A dinghy quickly relayed the men to the waiting PT boat. It was Sunday, August 8, exactly a week since they left Rendova harbor.

AFTERMATH

The men were treated at the local hospital. McMahon would recover from his burns. The others were returned to active duty.

John F. Kennedy was awarded the Navy and Marine Corps Medal and promoted to full lieutenant. He served again as the captain of a PT boat—PT 59. In October 1943, under enemy fire, his boat rescued a group of 60 marines.

But by November, Kennedy realized that his fighting days

were over. His back had been badly injured in the destruction of PT 109 and was strained more by towing McMahon. The injury would plague him the remainder of his life. The incident also had affected his adrenal glands. In the spring of 1944, Kennedy entered Chelsea Naval Hospital in Boston for medical treatment. That summer he was able, once again, to spend weekends with his family at Hyannis Port.

Politics was the furthest thing from Jack Kennedy's mind when he went into the Navy. He certainly didn't consider how his actions in the South Pacific would look to an electorate. But his heroic efforts in rescuing his crew were destined to become the stuff of legend and a rung on the ladder to political success.

Chapter 2
Born into Politics

Politics was in the Kennedy blood. It was inherited. If you were born in Boston and carried the name of Fitzgerald or Kennedy, politics was a way of life. John Fitzgerald Kennedy carried both names.

TOWARD A NEW LIFE

Both the Fitzgeralds and the Kennedys arrived in the United States from Ireland at about the same time—between 1848 and 1850. And both Patrick Kennedy and Thomas Fitzgerald came for the same reason, the Great Famine. In the fall of 1845, a fungus began to infect Ireland's most important crop, the potato. The exceptionally warm winter and the wet spring of 1846 caused the fungus blight to spread rapidly throughout the land and totally destroy the potato crop.

After two years of devastated crops and near starvation, thousands of Irishmen fled the country. For $20, they could get steerage-class passage to America. They traveled in the cargo areas of ships that were often called "coffin ships" because so many people died during the perilous journey. The American port to which the Cunard Shipping Line brought its passengers was Boston.

So many poor Irish Catholics flooded the Boston area that ethnic groups which had arrived earlier—the Scots, Scandinavians, and Germans—felt threatened. So did the Protestant Yankees, descendants of the Pilgrim founders of America. Signs that read "NINA" (No Irish Need Apply) appeared regularly at places of employment. Living in utter poverty and with few job prospects, the Irish found it almost impossible to break out of their desperate life in the slums of East Boston.

The Kennedy Way

Patrick Kennedy, great-grandfather of the future President, survived long enough to marry and father four children, the youngest of whom was named after his father. Shortly after young Patrick's birth, his father died. His mother was forced to work as a clerk in a shop to support the family.

Young Patrick found two ways to improve his lot and that of his family. He became a businessman and a politician. He saved enough money as a dockworker to open a saloon and later a wholesale liquor business. Patrick was not only a popular saloonkeeper, he was also a good listener. He listened to the complaints and problems of many a fellow Irishman and helped those who were down on their luck. He soon became a well-respected member of the community. The saloon became a hub for local politicians and, in time, campaign headquarters for Patrick himself.

He held a variety of offices, from state representative and state senator to fire commissioner and election commissioner. He also became a member of the unofficial Board of Strategy, a group of party bosses who picked candidates for the Democratic Party in Boston.

The Fitzgerald Way

While serving on the Board of Strategy, Patrick met John F. Kennedy's maternal grandfather, John Francis Fitzgerald. John Francis was one of the nine sons of Thomas Fitzgerald. Beginning as a fish peddler in the immigrant neighborhoods,

Thomas had saved enough money in six years to go into business with his brother, James. They opened a combination grocery, saloon, and liquor store and made enough money to go into the real estate business.

The Fitzgerald family fortunes improved so greatly that young John Francis was able to enter Boston's most historic high school, the Boston Latin School. The school had been established in 1635, just five years after the founding of Boston, and was the pride of proper Yankee Bostonians. John Francis did well enough at Boston Latin to be admitted to Harvard Medical School, but the death of his father forced him to leave before he could complete his studies.

Both of his parents were now gone, his oldest brother was struggling to raise his own family, and five of his younger brothers were still underage. Nevertheless, John Francis was determined to keep the family together. In desperation, he turned to Matthew Keany, the local Democratic ward boss. Keany suggested that John Francis go to work for him, and young Fitzgerald turned out to be a "natural" at politics.

Not long after that, John Francis began running for office—moving from city councilman to state legislator to United States congressman to mayor of Boston. With a ruddy round face, sparkling eyes, a ready wit, and a smooth manner, he became known as "Honey Fitz." More than one politician gave Honey Fitz credit for being a master of the "Irish switch": he could shake hands with one person while glibly talking with a second person.

Crossing Paths and Lives

Honey Fitz and Patrick Kennedy knew one another well. They were both members of what had become known as the "FIFs," the "First Irish Families." Yet it came as quite a surprise to many when Rose Fitzgerald, Honey Fitz's daughter, married Joseph Kennedy, Patrick's oldest son.

John Kennedy's two grandfathers, John F. Fitzgerald (left) and Patrick J. Kennedy, were friends who, in 1895, vacationed together in Asheville, North Carolina. (John F. Kennedy Library.)

Rose and Joseph had much in common—and one important difference. Both were Irish Catholics, both had fathers involved in Boston politics, and both were well-educated and ambitious. Rose had been greatly involved with her father on the political scene. After her graduation from Manhattanville College, she constantly accompanied him to rallies, banquets, grand marches, and Democratic Party conventions. Joseph Kennedy, on the other hand, wanted no part of politics. Early in his career, he told a reporter, "It doesn't make any difference how high a young man may rise in politics, nor how brilliant his future may seem, his ultimate defeat is inevitable."

Joseph had not forgotten his father's defeat in the race for street commissioner after eight terms in the state legislature. Nor had he forgotten that while at Harvard, he and other Irish Catholics had never been invited into its most prestigious clubs. Joseph Kennedy saw the way to social acceptance was by making money. Accordingly, on leaving Harvard, he went into banking, and by the age of 25, he was one of the country's youngest bank presidents.

Honey Fitz had not liked the strong, self-willed Joseph Kennedy as a husband for his favorite child, his "Wild Irish Rose." But Joseph's early financial success, and Rose's determination to marry him, left Honey Fitz with little choice. The couple was married in 1914 in a simple ceremony. A year later, their first son, Joseph, Jr., was born.

A GROWING FAMILY AND FORTUNE

John Fitzgerald Kennedy, their second son, was born on May 29, 1917, in the family home in Brookline, Massachusetts, one month after the United States entered World War I. At that time, Joseph Kennedy left the bank to become assistant general manager of the Bethlehem Steel shipyards in Quincy, Massachusetts. But before the war was over, Joseph already had his eye on bigger worlds to conquer. He saw that the stock market was the place to become a millionaire.

Joseph had just begun a new career as a stockbroker in Boston when he was forced to give his full attention to his family. Young John, now affectionately known as "Jack," was near death from scarlet fever, at that time a frightful and very contagious disease. Because Rose was recovering from the birth of their fourth child, it was Joseph who had to nurse Jack day and night.

Jack ran temperatures as high as 105 degrees, and his condition seemed to grow worse each day. In desperation,

With the marriage of Joseph Kennedy and Rose Fitzgerald in October 1914, two of the "First Irish Families" in Boston were merged. (Boston Globe.)

Joseph used all his influence to get the boy admitted to Boston City Hospital, even though the hospital's 125 beds in the isolation section were already filled. Sitting at Jack's bedside, Joseph began to realize that no amount of money could pay for the loss of his son.

It took more than three months before Jack returned home. The hospital nurses recall that he was a delightful and charming child, with whom it was easy to work up a special relationship. Perhaps because he was younger and smaller than Joseph, Jr., Jack had found other ways to gain attention.

With the arrival of a third brother, Robert, in 1925, there were now seven children in the family. Two more, Jean and Edward, would follow. With such a large clan to look after, nurses, governesses, and other domestic help were also a regular part of the family.

The Model Kennedy

After Kennedy began investing in a new industry, filmmaking, he often had to go to Hollywood on business. But when he came home, he always became deeply involved with his family. At dinner, he would raise topics for discussion, mostly dealing with American government and politics. When Jack's father was out of town, his mother, Rose Kennedy, would preside over the mealtime discussions. The one subject *never* discussed was money.

Joseph Kennedy was a model of what he expected of his children, a passionate loyalty to family and an acute sense of competition. Because Joseph and his family were often made to feel like "outsiders," especially by Boston society, the family gained a feeling of "the Kennedys against the world," and the children became fiercely loyal to one another. Competition was natural in such a large clan, but in the case of the Kennedys, it was an important part of their upbringing. They were raised to compete and to finish first. Rose Kennedy once remarked, "My husband is quite a strict father; he likes the boys to win at sports and everything they try. If they don't win, he will discuss their failure with them, but he doesn't have much patience with the loser."

The same spirit that had made the early Kennedys and Fitzgeralds strive to better their station in life became the driving force for Joseph Kennedy's family. "Winning," whether in sports, business, or politics, was essential. Second place was just not good enough.

Chapter 3
The Education of a Kennedy

It was 1932. In the heart of the Great Depression, the enormous economic collapse that gripped America in the 1930s, one out of every four workers was unemployed. Long lines of hungry people waited at "soup kitchens" to be fed. Men lined up early in the day at employment offices hoping to get a day's work. Wages and farm prices had dropped dramatically.

But the world of the Kennedy children was far removed from the unpleasant world outside. Summers were spent at Cape Cod, in the family's big, 10-bedroom home at Hyannis Port. And when most Americans were struggling to meet rent or mortgage payments, Joseph Kennedy bought his family a huge, rambling, Spanish-style waterfront estate in Palm Beach, Florida, as their winter vacation home.

SIBLING RIVALRIES

At home, Joe, Jr., had taken on more than the role of just "big brother." With Joseph, Sr., away so much of the time, young Joe had to be the "man of the house." Whereas Jack was lanky and underweight, Joe, Jr., was husky and athletic. Jack soon learned he could not win in the wrestling matches in which the two brothers often engaged.

All of the Kennedy children attended private schools because their father wanted them to meet the children of the "right people." Jack first attended private schools in Boston, then, at the age of 13, he spent a year at Canterbury, a Catholic boarding school in New Milford, Connecticut. The following year he entered Choate, an Episcopal prep school in Wallingford, Connecticut, where his older brother was already enrolled. This marked the beginning of the many times that Jack would follow in Joe, Jr.'s, steps.

At Choate, Jack became best friends with LeMoyne "Lem" Billings, with whom he shared a common problem, older brothers who were great achievers. However, both young men decided, perhaps unconsciously, not to compete scholastically with their brothers, but to win friends and influence people with their own charm and humor.

Jack's teachers deplored his lack of perseverance in his studies, but they agreed that he was bright. When he found a subject that really interested him, Jack would delve into it with serious questions and enthusiasm. But grades never really seemed to be important to him.

A Puzzling Personality

Jack was also a matter of concern to his parents. He would upset his mother by arriving late to meals, and he tended to be sloppy about his clothes and forgetful about many things. Yet she knew he was perhaps more intelligent than Joe, Jr. During times when he was ill, he would read for hours. His tastes ranged from *Peter Pan* to Kipling's *Jungle Books*, *Treasure Island*, and *King Arthur and the Knights of the Round Table*.

To his father, Jack was a puzzle. How could a young man who read the *New York Times* newspaper from front to back each day be so lazy about school work? How could a young man who had to overcome so many physical ailments have such a drive to succeed in sports? At Choate, for example, Jack went out for baseball, basketball, the rowing team, and golf. And why did he prefer the role of prankster to scholar?

For Jack could not resist a good joke. In his senior year, he faced expulsion from Choate for his role in helping Lem and 10 other friends form the "Muckers' Club." On several occasions, the headmaster had talked about "muckers," students who did not follow the rules and who "goofed-off" instead of taking their studies seriously. The kinds of things that Jack's group did were nothing more serious than playing the radio after hours and sneaking out for milk shakes. But when the group arrived with special badges announcing their allegiance to the club, the headmaster was forced to notify Jack's father.

When he was summoned to the headmaster's office, Jack was fearful about what his father would say and do. However, a sly wink from Joseph Kennedy assured his son that he was on his side. But after he heard the complaints of the headmaster, Joseph assured him that he would support the school's actions.

At lunch later, with kindly wit, Joseph told Jack that he did not approve of his behavior, and he hoped it would be a good lesson for Jack. It seemed to be. Jack was not expelled. He also realized the depth of his father's support and was not about to risk losing it again. His grades improved, and when he graduated later that year, he ranked in the middle of his class.

Schools, Schools, Illnesses, Illnesses

While at Choate, Jack enjoyed frequent meetings with his sister, Kathleen, who attended a nearby Catholic school. Known in the family as "Kick," Kathleen was the sister closest in age to Jack. She was vivacious, a beautiful girl, had great personal charm, and shared with Jack a wild sense of humor.

Following his graduation from Choate, Jack was offered

the opportunity to study at the University of London with Harold Laski, a renowned professor of political science. Kathleen was sent to school in France. Their parents knew how close the two children were and hoped that they would enjoy holidays together.

Jack had barely begun his studies in London when he became seriously ill with an attack of jaundice and had to return to the United States. By early October, though he was still not well and classes had already started, his father managed to get Jack admitted into Princeton. But a few weeks after Thanksgiving, he was forced by illness to leave Princeton.

After two months in the hospital, Jack was sent to a ranch in Arizona, owned by one of his father's friends. The warm sun and dry climate helped him regain his health. By the fall of 1936, Jack was ready to return to school. This time, he agreed to follow his father's and his brother's footsteps by enrolling at Harvard.

The lanky six-footer who entered Harvard in 1936 weighed 149 pounds. As at Choate, Jack was determined to earn his letters as an athlete. But at a football scrimmage during his sophomore year, he received a back injury that would plague him for the rest of his life. He also worked out on the swimming team and hoped to make the squad for an important meet with Yale. Illness, however, intervened once again, and he was sent to the school infirmary. Nevertheless, he managed to sneak into the school pool to work out an hour a day, but in the qualifying heat, he lost by three seconds.

Jack had no better success with his attempts at campus politics. While brother Joe served three terms on the Student Council and became chairman in his senior year, Jack's attempts at winning a place on the council or becoming class president proved futile.

INTERNATIONAL AFFAIRS

Following his freshman year at Harvard, Jack and Lem Billings, his friend from Choate, spent the summer touring France, Italy, Germany, Holland, and England. His father encouraged his two older sons to travel abroad, possibly because of his own new interest in politics and international affairs.

As the Depression deepened and the 1932 election year rolled around, Joseph Kennedy began to worry about the economic and social conditions in the United States. Because he felt it was important that the nation be led by a strong President, he decided to support Franklin D. Roosevelt, the Democratic candidate.

In return for his support, after the election President Roosevelt appointed Joseph Kennedy the chairman of the newly created Securities and Exchange Commission. Following criticism and concerns about careless or dishonest business operations that might have led to the stock market crash of 1929, Congress had decided that all security exchanges should be under government regulation. Kennedy was the first chairman of the new commission.

In 1937, one of Joseph Kennedy's greatest dreams came true. He was the first American Irishman to be appointed ambassador to England. For the Kennedy clan, it opened doors to the international scene and international society.

An Awakening

During his first two years at Harvard, Jack showed little interest in what was happening in the world. When other students were talking about the civil war in Spain and the menace of Hitler in Germany, Jack remained aloof. But when he began his junior year, in the fall of 1938, he became so intrigued with what was happening in Europe that he received permission from his father to spend the second semester of that year in London.

The entire family was there, making quite a sensation. For Jack, his brother Joe, and sister "Kick," the social whirl was tremendously exciting. But Jack wanted more than that. Instead of remaining in London, he traveled to Paris, Poland, Germany, Latvia, the Balkans, Russia, Turkey, and Palestine.

By the time Jack returned to Harvard in the fall of 1939, his attitude toward scholarship had changed so dramatically that his final paper for graduation earned him a *magna cum laude* in political science. The paper, called "Why England Slept," described the meetings in September 1938 of English Prime Minister Neville Chamberlain with the German leader, Adolph Hitler. These meetings resulted in an agreement that would bring only temporary peace in Europe. Jack's father was so impressed with his son's work that he had it published as a book. It became a best-seller and earned Jack his first national and international notice.

In approving his son's travels during the spring of 1939, Jack's father directed him to send written reports about the countries he visited and the people he met. Jack's letters to his father revealed that he was a careful observer. For example, he found Russia to be "a crude and backward country," and he gave an impartial analysis of the conflict between the Jewish population and the Arabs in Palestine.

Creeping Shadow of War

In London, despite Chamberlain's peace mission to Germany, Ambassador Kennedy could see war coming to Europe. Because he hoped that the United States would not allow itself to be drawn into such a war, people called him an "isolationist."

On September 1, 1939, German tanks rolled across the Polish border, destroying the 12 brigades of cavalry oppos-

The three oldest Kennedy children, Joe, Jr. (left), Kathleen (Kick), and Jack, in London in September 1939. They are shown on their way to the House of Commons to hear Great Britain declare war on Germany. By 1948, Jack would be the sole survivor of the "golden trio." (John F. Kennedy Library.)

ing them. Two days later, Joseph Kennedy was called to a private meeting with British Prime Minister Chamberlain. Afterward, the ambassador immediately telephoned President Roosevelt, relaying the news that England would be declaring war on Germany. "It's the end of the world," he kept repeating, "it's the end of everything."

That same night, Ambassador Kennedy was awakened from his sleep. A British ship, the *Athenia*, had been torpedoed on its way to the United States. It carried 300 American passengers. The American survivors were sent to Glasgow, Scotland, and Ambassador Kennedy sent Jack there to assist the survivors in any way he could. This experience gave Jack his first look at what war was like.

By the end of September 1939, Jack and the other family members had returned to the safety of the United States. Now London was under nightly air attacks, and the family was very worried about Joseph Kennedy. He, too, was anxious to be reunited with his wife and children.

Ambassador Kennedy continued to argue strongly that the United States should not become involved in "Europe's War." His comments so displeased President Roosevelt that he ordered the ambassador to return to the United States. He arrived just in time to make a campaign speech on the radio in support of President Roosevelt. Then, on November 4, 1940, Franklin Delano Roosevelt was elected to an unprecedented third term as President of the United States.

Yet Joseph Kennedy continued to side with the isolationists. In the spring, shortly after his inauguration, President Roosevelt declared a "state of emergency." Despite his father's sentiments—with which he agreed—Joe, Jr., left law school and enlisted in the Naval Air Cadets. Jack, too, wanted to enter military service.

Chapter 4
Following the Family Tradition

Jack Kennedy returned to the family home in Hyannis Port in the summer of 1944, just as tragedy struck a double blow. On August 2, exactly one year after the destruction of PT 109, the Kennedy family learned that Joe, Jr.'s plane had exploded while he was on a secret mission over the coast of Europe. A month later, the husband of Jack's sister, "Kick," was killed in battle. Compounding these emotional shocks, Jack was recovering from an unsuccessful back operation.

In April 1945, Franklin Delano Roosevelt, now in his fourth term as President, died just three months after his inauguration. That same month, with help from his father, Jack Kennedy was assigned by the Hearst newspapers to write about the first United Nations Conference in San Francisco. The reports that Jack sent back to his editor were quite profound. He believed in the need for such a world organization. Yet he saw enough political shenanigans going on to realize that politics could eventually destroy the purpose of the United Nations. Many would later feel that he was correct in his prediction.

The war in Europe was coming to an end. And in August 1945, Japan accepted an unconditional surrender after two of its cities were hit by atomic bombs. World War II was over.

Back from the Navy, Jack (left) and Bobby (center) join young Edward (Ted) Kennedy at the family home in Hyannis Port in 1946. (John F. Kennedy Library.)

A POLITICAL LIFE BEGINS

It was a time of decision for Jack Kennedy. Joe, Jr.'s, death left a strange void in Jack's life. His older brother had been his model and his chief competitor—in sports, in academic achievement, and even for the affection of his parents. Their father had made known his ambitions for his oldest son: Joe, Jr., was going to be the first Irish Catholic President of the United States. As for Jack, he might do well as a writer or a historian.

Money was not a problem. Jack's father had arranged a trust fund for each of his children. As Jack said, "I didn't need to make money or go into business." He thought about going into "public service."

The world of politics beckoned, but Jack hesitated taking the plunge. He did not consider himself much of a public speaker. He tended to be shy with people outside of his own social circle. Honey Fitz had shown him enough of the "blarney"–the handshaking and the backslapping that went with traditional campaigning. That was not for him.

But fate stepped in–in the guise of James Michael Curley, one-time mayor of Boston, opponent of Honey Fitz, and now the congressman from the 11th District in East Boston. Curley had been defeated in his run for governor and for the Senate. Now, as his days dwindled, he wanted to come home, to be mayor of Boston once more.

The First Run

In November 1945, Curley won the election for mayor. His congressional seat was now open. Nine candidates filed for the Democratic primary, including Jack Kennedy, who had been persuaded by others to do so. Whoever won the Democratic nomination would be the new congressman, for the 11th District was a Democratic stronghold.

Jack was hardly a commanding figure as a candidate. Though six feet tall, he was a scrawny 140 pounds and only 28 years old. His opponents called him a "poor little rich kid." Moreover, he was a "carpetbagger," an outsider who knew little about the people he hoped to represent. He was also such a rank amateur that he almost forgot to file his nomination papers.

But Jack was a fast learner. First of all, he was determined to bring a sense of dignity to the campaign. He did not attack his opponents. He learned what the people wanted and he spoke about those issues—jobs, Social Security, veterans' benefits, and housing.

The nucleus of his support came from old friends like Lem Billings, from his younger brother, Bob, just out of the Navy, and from a group of young Democrats who lived in the 11th District. One of them was Dave Powers.

At the suggestion of a local politician, Kennedy went to meet Powers on a bitter cold evening in January 1946. Climbing the steps of a three-story tenement, he found the young veteran sipping beer. Dave Powers explained that he was pretty well committed to another candidate. But Jack persisted and invited Dave to a meeting of Gold Star Mothers— women who had lost sons in the war. As Jack finished his speech, which lasted only 10 minutes, he turned to the audience and said softly, "I think I know how all you mothers feel. You see, my mother is a Gold Star Mother, too." There was not a dry eye in the hall.

Dave Powers was overwhelmed by the way the audience crowded around the candidate to touch his hand and to talk to him. When Jack later asked him whether he would consider helping with his campaign, Dave exclaimed, "I'm already working for you." He would continue to work with Jack till the final days at the White House.

Reaching for Resources

Traditional politicians generally work with their party members almost exclusively, but Kennedy reached out. No matter that Lem Billings was a Republican. If you wanted to help, you were welcomed into the fold, and a job was found. Volunteers, smitten by the charm of their candidate, soon converted friends and relatives.

Nor did Jack overlook the talents of his own family. His father worked behind the scenes. On many a night, father and son would review the day's events and Jack's speeches.

Joe Kennedy was Jack's most enthusiastic supporter. Jack once told a friend, "If I walked out on the stage and fell flat on my face, Father would say I fell better than anyone else."

In order to establish residence in the 11th Congressional District, Jack set up his headquarters at the Bellevue Hotel, just down the hall from where Honey Fitz lived. Grandpa Fitz helped out by making speeches and was a big hit with the senior citizens. When Jack decided that he had to reach out to the people in their communities, sisters Eunice and Pat worked with local volunteer hostesses to hold parties. The two sisters would provide cups and saucers, cookies and coffee, and "warm up the crowd" until Jack arrived. With good luck, Jack could make as many as four or five appearances in an evening.

His mother, Rose, an "old pro" from her campaign days with her father, proved to be a star in the constellation of supporters. She always arrived at a meeting elegantly dressed. She would not discuss political issues. Instead, she told stories about the family and the glamorous years at court in England. Her audience loved it as she spoke about the king, queen, and other celebrities she had met.

The Campaign Routine

As the campaign gained momentum, Jack's days took on a set routine. Often, even before daylight, he would be at the waterfront greeting dockworkers, or standing at plant gates shaking hands with factory workers. After breakfast at a diner, he would drop into tenements and introduce himself to surprised housewives. Later in the day, he might be found in such places as fire stations, markets, barbershops, or taverns, meeting voters.

This "getting out to meet the people" had not been done before in Boston. When he started, Kennedy was not sure that he would like the personal approach. But once into the swing of the campaign, Jack began to really enjoy himself. Even the night before the election, he was still campaigning. He was in a car with friends when Jack spied an elderly woman trying to cross the street. "Stop the car," he called out. Then he ran over to the woman and helped her across the street. As he got back into the car, one of the men in the back blurted out, "You *really* do want every vote, don't you?"

But the strenuous campaign effort aggravated Jack's back pain. His associates soon found that the best time to talk to him was before dinner, when he was in the bathtub. A long, hot bath seemed to relieve the pain. A friend, William Manchester, commented, "With the possible exception of Winston Churchill, Jack may have taken more baths than any politician in history."

When the primary election returns came in on June 18, 1946, it was evident that Kennedy had won a smashing victory. That night, Grandpa Honey Fitz celebrated by jumping up on a table, dancing an Irish jig, and singing "Sweet Adeline," the song from his own campaign days. In November, Jack won the congressional seat by a landslide.

Political and Personal Independence

On January 3, 1947, Jack Kennedy took the congressman's oath and immediately set himself on his own road. He defied tradition by not meeting with the senior Massachusetts congressman, John W. McCormack, to pledge allegiance to the head of the state's Democratic Party. And although he was a new member on the House of Representatives' Education and Labor Committee, he started out by criticizing President Truman's trade policy.

Jack also refused to sign a petition for Mayor Curley's pardon. During his fourth term as mayor of Boston, Curley was found guilty of mail fraud and sentenced to jail. Yet the people of Boston still supported him, and more than one-

Three generations—Jack's grandfather, Honey Fitz (left), and his father—celebrate Jack Kennedy's victory in his first political venture in June 1946. After winning the Democratic primary in the Democratic 11th Congressional District of Boston, he was assured of election to the U.S. House of Representatives. (John F. Kennedy Library.)

quarter of them signed petitions asking for clemency. McCormack himself sought a pardon for Curley from President Truman.

Many of Kennedy's staff members urged him not to cross McCormack, but it was a difficult situation for Jack. He could not bring himself to seek leniency for a convicted criminal, especially one who was an enemy of Honey Fitz. His grandfather had been forced out of Boston politics when Curley defeated him in a mayoral race.

After Kennedy publicly announced that he would not support a pardon for Curley, he returned to his office and admitted, "I'm dead now, politically finished." The press singled him out as the only Democratic congressman from Massachusetts who did not endorse a Curley pardon. But the public reaction was very different from what was expected. People saw Kennedy as a maverick. Here was a new breed of Irish politician, a man who was independent, with a mind of his own, who was better educated and better bred.

Yet Kennedy was a freshman congressman in many ways. Not only was he one of the youngest and newest members in the House of Representatives, he looked so boyish that one of the lobbyists persisted in calling him "Laddie." His casual attire did not help his image. He wore old khaki pants, often with his shirt-tail hanging out. While other congressmen went home to their families in the evening, Kennedy might be found playing a pick-up game of football or softball with boys in the local playground. They had no idea that the young man in the dirty gym shoes and a shabby shirt was a congressman. He also spent time reading, seeing movies, and, like any red-blooded male, dating girls.

POSITIONS, PROSPECTS, AND PAIN

In the spring and summer of 1947, the big issue in Washington was the Marshall Plan. At the urging of Secretary of State George C. Marshall, President Truman and Congress were considering a plan to offer considerable financial aid to the ruined economies of Europe. Such action was unprecedented in history. Earlier, defeated enemies were asked to pay reparations, large sums of money for the damages inflicted on the winning nation. Now, in an effort to halt the spread of Communism, the United States was offering to help such former enemies as West Germany and Italy, as well as such allies as Britain and France.

As part of a congressional fact-finding committee, Kennedy traveled to Russia and western Europe to learn more about education and labor conditions there. On the same trip, he visited with his sister, Kick, in Ireland and went to New Ross to find his roots. There, in the town from which his family had emigrated, Kennedy found several members of his family clan.

Disease and Death

On his return to London, Jack collapsed. The illness was diagnosed as Addison's disease, a failure of the adrenal glands. For the press, the Kennedy family called it a recurrence of malaria, from his days in the South Pacific. The public was always shielded from knowledge about Jack's poor health. However, because of his illness, he had the worst attendance record in the House.

The staff worked hard to compensate for Kennedy's illness. They made sure he read up on all the important issues and that the problems of his constituents in Boston were attended to promptly. In Boston, his public seemed well satisfied with their representative.

In May of 1948, Kick was killed in a plane accident. The tragedy affected all the family, but it hit Jack particularly hard. The visit with her the previous summer had been special for both of them. She had been so young and full of vitality. And now she, like Joe, Jr., had died at an early age. Of the three oldest children—Joe, Jr., Kathleen, and Jack—Jack, at the age of 31, was the only one left.

For a while, the thought of death haunted Kennedy. The loss of his two siblings and his own illness made him speak often about the subject to close friends. Just about this time, however, a new drug was discovered for treating Addison's disease. As his health began to improve, so did Kennedy's spirits.

Looking Ahead

Back in action once more, Kennedy's voting record in Congress left his observers confused. He did not vote the Democratic line, nor did he always vote the way his father thought. As a congressman, he voted in favor of several issues on which he would later change his opinions. Like his father, he was anti-Communist. But in voting for the Marshall Plan, he contradicted his father's isolationist feelings. He earned a reputation as a supporter of low-income housing and federal aid to education.

Jack was re-elected to Congress in 1948 and again in 1950 in landslide victories. But the job itself was not satisfying. As one of 435 members of the House, he was a small fish in a big pond. He relished running for office—the meeting with tradesmen and secretaries, dockworkers and housewives—but for a man whose health was a chronic concern, the experience of running every two years was exhausting. In addition, he was finding the job rather boring.

Shortly after his victory in 1950, he began seeking statewide recognition. He had his eyes on a bigger political prize, either governor or senator. In early 1952, when the governor of Massachusetts decided to run for a second term, Kennedy focused on the state's senatorial seat, which would be up for election that year.

Now he was facing a respected and experienced opponent. The incumbent senator was Henry Cabot Lodge, Jr., a Yankee from one of Boston's best-known and oldest families, a man who had been elected to the Senate three times, and who had credentials as a World War II veteran.

But Kennedy's organization was well-prepared. It had learned much from the three earlier campaigns for the House. His supporters gathered lists of all the special interest groups—from insurance men and Albanian Americans to college professors and taxi drivers. Jewish newspapers carried Kennedy's greetings and a message for the Jewish New Year. Reprints of articles about Kennedy's PT 109 experience were left as free reading materials at hair salons and barbershops. Researchers collected data comparing Kennedy's record and Lodge's. And for the first time, the new communication medium, television, was used with great success.

Unsung Issues

On two occasions, Kennedy and Lodge debated each other in a gentlemanly and pleasant fashion. There was no mud-slinging. They even said nice things about each other. And though they discussed many of the issues of state and local politics, neither candidate brought up two of the biggest national issues, the Korean War and McCarthyism.

When, in 1950, North Koreans crossed the demarcation line separating their divided country and invaded South Korea, United Nations troops were sent to halt the Communist invasion.

Most of these troops and commanders were Americans. On the issue of Korea, Jack and his father had differing opinions. Joseph Kennedy felt that the United States could not hope to defend and hold Korea or any other place in Asia. Jack's concern was that the defense of Korea should not take American troops away from other important areas, such as West Germany.

In October 1951 Jack went on a tour of the Far East. Though he became very ill in Japan and had to cut the trip short, he returned with a fresh point of view. He realized that

When John F. Kennedy ran for the Senate in 1952, his mother, Rose, was a tireless campaigner. She had learned to charm the crowds while campaigning for her father, Honey Fitz, and continued to win votes when her son ran for office. (John F. Kennedy Library.)

nationalism was a greater force than communism, that countries were more interested in ridding themselves of colonial domination than they were in adopting communism.

McCarthyism was a more delicate issue. Joseph McCarthy, a senator from Wisconsin, was a fanatic anti-Communist.

During the 1950s, he accused many innocent people of being "Reds" or of having associated with Communists although he failed to back the charges with supporting evidence. He trampled on civil liberties, and damaged reputations and careers through lies and innuendos.

Neither Kennedy nor Lodge wished to tackle the issue of McCarthyism because no state had a higher proportion of McCarthy supporters than Massachusetts. But liberals expected Kennedy to take a stand against McCarthy. However, Kennedy finally decided to take the advice of his father, who cautioned his son to wait. "If you have to make a tough choice," counseled Joseph Kennedy, "let the other man make it."

Senator Lodge eventually did endorse McCarthy in order to satisfy conservative Republicans. It may very well have cost him the election. But other factors may have been more important.

With financial backing from family and friends, Kennedy was able to outspend Lodge for radio, billboards, and newspaper ads. A big television campaign played up the charisma of Jack Kennedy—his youth, glamor, humor, and smile. And since early 1952, even before he knew that he would be running for a seat in the Senate, Kennedy had started to acquire a statewide reputation by speaking in almost all of the 351 cities and towns in Massachusetts.

By election night, Kennedy was calm and confident. The Republicans won both the governorship in Massachusetts and the presidency. But Democrat Kennedy beat Republican Lodge by 70,000 votes. It was exactly 36 years since Henry Cabot Lodge, Sr., had defeated Jack Kennedy's grandfather for the Senate. It was too bad that Honey Fitz missed that election night, but he had died two years before. He would have loved celebrating his grandson's victory with an Irish jig.

Chapter 5

The Senator Takes a Wife and a Gamble

"**S**tand back and let the senators go first," barked the guard. He put out his arm to hold back the scrawny, tousle-headed fellow trying to get on the subway that runs between the House and the Senate.

Who could blame the guard for not recognizing the new senator? In January 1953, Jack Kennedy was only 36 years old and looked like 26. Senators tended to be older, heavier, and grayer. At a time when Republicans had swept Dwight D. Eisenhower into the White House and taken control of Congress, Jack, a Democrat, had managed to defeat a seasoned and highly respected Republican senator. John Fitzgerald Kennedy was no longer just a "rich man's son."

A "SPASMODIC COURTSHIP"

In fact, he was beginning to resent the image that many people still had of him as a playboy. An article in the *Saturday Evening Post* magazine that spring was titled "The Senate's Gay Young Bachelor." In it, Jack was called "the most eligible bachelor in the United States" who drove around Washington in "his long convertible, hatless and with the car's top down." One writer said he was "an informal, casual millionaire who caused women in the galleries to swoon."

Perhaps it was time to settle down. After all, his younger brother, Bobby, was already married and a father. And that spring, his sister, Eunice, was going to get married. Also, he was now dating a very charming young woman.

When Senator John Kennedy arrived for President Eisenhower's Inaugural Ball on January 20, 1953, on his arm was a beautifully gowned young woman with dark hair, dark-brown eyes with long lashes, and an enchanting smile. Her name was Jacqueline Bouvier. Only 23 years old, "Jackie" was a photographer for a Washington newspaper. She came from a wealthy Catholic family, well-known in society. She had studied at Vassar, the Sorbonne in Paris, and had recently received a degree from George Washington University in Washington, D.C.

In 1952, mutual friends, newspaperman Charles Bartlett and his wife Martha, invited Jack and Jackie to dinner. As they were leaving, Jack asked her for a date. Before she could reply, they discovered a boyfriend of Jackie's crouched in the back seat of her car. She shrugged her shoulders, as if to say, "What can I do?"—and Jack left in a huff.

But he was interested. Learning from Bartlett that Jackie spoke Spanish, Italian, and French fluently, he called her to translate some French documents dealing with the struggle going on in Indo-China (Vietnam). She did. However, because Jack was busy running for the Senate seat against Lodge, six months passed without a date.

When he returned to Washington, Jack began what Jackie called "a very spasmodic courtship." He took her dancing and to the movies. His favorites were westerns and Civil War films. He was not the flowers and candy type, but he did send her books. Most of the courtship was conducted from phone booths in Massachusetts, where he spent part of each week. Nor did he ever send a love letter—the only mail being a card from Bermuda with the one line, "Wish you were here."

In May 1953, while Jackie was in London photographing the coronation of Queen Elizabeth II, Jack proposed by telegram. Jackie accepted but she was a bit miffed that they did not announce their engagement until after June 13th, when the magazine article about the "gay young bachelor" appeared.

The wedding took place on September 12, 1953, at St. Mary's Roman Catholic Church in Newport, Rhode Island. It was an American version of a royal wedding. The *Boston Globe* called it "one of the most notable weddings in this old and fashionable resort." Archbishop Cushing of Boston performed the ceremony and read a special blessing that had been sent by Pope Pius XII. More than 1,200 guests attended the reception on the magnificent 300-acre estate of Jackie's stepfather, Hugh Auchincloss. Among the invited guests were business tycoons, socialites, members of Congress, and ambassadors.

The bride was exquisite in a taffeta gown and lace veil. The groom was tall, handsome, and elegant, but those who got a close-up look of him could not help noticing the long, red scratches on his face. Jack had spent the day before his wedding in one of the family's notorious touch-football games and had plunged headlong into a briar patch.

FIRST DAYS IN THE SENATE

Jack liked the move to the Senate. It had a tradition that appealed to his sense of history. Daily he walked past the statues of such historic predecessors as Henry Clay and Daniel Webster. He liked being a colleague to men he had met through his father, such as Lyndon B. Johnson, leader of the Democratic minority, and Robert A. Taft, "Mr. Republican," who was the majority leader.

Jack's first two years in the Senate were spent keeping his promises to his Massachusetts' constituents. He helped

46 *John F. Kennedy*

John F. Kennedy and his bride, Jacqueline Lee Bouvier, on their wedding day, September 12, 1953, in Newport, Rhode Island. It was hailed as one of the most glamorous weddings ever held in this New England resort town. (John F. Kennedy Library.)

pass tariffs (taxes on imports) to protect the fishing, watch, and textile industries, thereby increasing the cost of foreign goods. He suggested to his New England colleagues a regional approach to legislation to help more than Massachusetts. That gained him the support of congressmen from nearby states in bringing jobs and flood-control measures into the area.

Illness Strikes Again

There never seemed to be a time when Jack Kennedy was completely free from pain or illness. But during his second year as senator, the pain in his back became so unbearable that he was forced to use crutches to relieve the pressure on his back.

In August, after Congress had recessed for the summer, he met with a team of doctors who suggested a complicated and risky operation. They hoped a fusion of two discs in his spine would relieve the pain. But they warned that since he suffered from Addison's disease, he would be at great peril because he had such a poor resistance to infections. His father tried to talk him out of the surgery. He reminded Jack that Franklin D. Roosevelt had managed the presidency from a wheelchair. But Jack decided to go ahead.

Three days after the operation, he did get an infection. Antibiotics had no effect. His condition became so critical that the family was called to his bedside. Joseph Kennedy was sure his son was dying. A priest was called to give Jack the last rites of the Catholic Church, but he managed to pull through. For months afterward, however, he remained in poor physical condition.

McCarthy Condemned

On December 2, the Senate voted on a motion to condemn Senator McCarthy for his unfounded accusations of communism in the army and the way he had trampled on the liberties of innocent citizens. Though he personally found McCarthy's actions a disgrace to the Senate, Jack was in a quandary. Many people in Massachusetts still supported McCarthy's stand on communism—and so did his father. Though ill and still in the hospital, Senator Kennedy could have informed the Senate of his vote by sending a message to a member of his staff in Washington.

Rather than take a stand, however, Kennedy used his illness as an excuse and remained silent. The Senate voted 67-22 to condemn McCarthy. Kennedy's silence on the subject would come back to haunt him later.

Profiles in Courage

Though it had been several months since his surgery, Jack's condition was still poor. In February 1955, he returned to the hospital for more surgery. This time the operation was successful. Though ill and in pain much of the time, Jack could not remain inactive. During his months in the hospital, he kept in touch with his Washington staff, he read, and he began to write a book.

Jack wanted to relate the true stories of men who had served in the Senate and who had the courage to stand up for what they believed was the nation's need, even though it cost them their popularity and, at times, their place in the Senate. Among the senators he praised were John Quincy Adams, Daniel Webster, and Edmund Ross, who cast the deciding vote against the impeachment of President Andrew Johnson.

When published in 1956, the book, *Profiles in Courage*, became a best-seller. Jack was hailed as an author and, in 1957, he was awarded the highest award given in the United States to an author, the Pulitzer Prize.

Many critics questioned whether Kennedy had actually written the book alone. But many friends who had visited him in the hospital during his illness said they saw Jack lying flat on his back with a board and a yellow pad propped up before him, writing his notes. There is little doubt that Jack received help, particularly from the man who became his legislative assistant in 1953 and later his Special Counsel to the President—Theodore C. Sorensen. But as one columnist observed, "This kind of political production is normal, not only for an officeholder's speeches but for his books."

What is probably of more importance is why Kennedy chose the subject he did. His brother, Bobby, once wrote that Jack Kennedy admired courage most of all. Certainly Jack had proven his physical courage in the war and in his battles with illness. Whether he had the moral courage to risk his career for a belief was debatable. The coming years would test this kind of courage.

RETURN TO THE FRAY

After being away for seven months, Kennedy returned to Washington on May 23, 1955. In his office was a huge basket of fruit. The card read, "Welcome home." It was signed, "Dick Nixon," then the Vice-President of the United States. When he entered the Senate chamber, his colleagues stood up and applauded. Though his family hoped he would take it easy, he plunged immediately into action; 1956 was going to be a presidential election year and Kennedy's goals had expanded once more.

Now he wanted to be a figure on the national scene. And this time, the ambition, the drive, seemed to come from within himself. It was as if he no longer had to prove himself to his father—or to live out his father's dream for Joe, Jr. The bug had bitten him. He had the organization, the people, and the self-confidence.

He began by defeating William Burke as chairman of the Massachusetts delegation to the Democratic National Convention. It was the first time Jack had done battle not for his own candidacy, but to gain control of the party machinery. Now he had to make up his mind whether he should make a run for the vice-presidency.

His father strongly opposed the idea. He felt the party's candidate would be Adlai Stevenson, former governor of Illinois, who would go down in defeat to Eisenhower, just as he had in 1952. He argued that if Jack were the nominee for Vice-President, the defeat would be attributed to a Catholic being on the ticket. That might permanently kill Jack's chances of ever running for President.

Others felt that even if he failed to win the nomination, Jack would be viewed by the country as a national figure. Although he made no decision concerning the nomination, Jack let it be known that if others wanted to line up support for him, he would not object.

The 1956 Democratic Convention

When the convention opened in August in Chicago, Jack Kennedy got a running start. He had been asked to narrate a film on the history of the Democratic Party. After it was shown at the convention, Jack appeared on the platform, setting off the convention's first enthusiastic demonstration for a potential candidate.

Except for one incident, Jack's chances looked good. He had visited Eleanor Roosevelt, widow of the late President, Franklin D. Roosevelt. She was influential among the party's intellectuals. Her first question to Jack was, "And where do you stand on McCarthyism?" Though he said he approved the Senate's condemnation vote, his response did not satisfy Mrs. Roosevelt. When she hurried off, Jack realized he could not count on her support.

It is customary for a presidential candidate to choose his Vice-President. On the second night of the convention, Stevenson requested that Jack deliver the speech nominating Stevenson as the Democratic candidate for the presidency.

Hearing this, Jack was sure Stevenson was offering him a consolation prize; if he won, Stevenson had another choice in mind for his running mate. Nevertheless, Kennedy and Ted Sorensen worked through the night to prepare the speech. Stevenson won on the first ballot.

"Go For It!"

Then Stevenson stunned the delegates. In a brief speech, he explained, "The American people have the solemn obligation to consider with the utmost care who will be their President if the elected President is prevented by a higher will from serving a full term.

"In these circumstances I have concluded to depart from the precedents of the past. I have decided that the selection of the vice-presidential nominee should be made through the free process of this convention."

The convention was in an uproar. What had seemed to be a rather dull convention had suddenly become a free-for-all. The candidates had only about 12 hours until the balloting for the vice-presidency began.

The session began at noon the next day. Thirteen names were put into nomination. At the end of the first ballot, Senator Estes Kefauver of Tennessee was clearly in the lead with 483½ votes. Kennedy had 304 votes. The magic number needed to win the nomination was 686.

In his hotel, Jack watched the proceedings on television. On the second ballot, he grabbed the lead, 618 to Kefauver's 551½. And then he began to notice excited groups down on the floor. Suddenly, Senator Albert Gore of Tennessee, a candidate himself for the vice-presidential nomination, shouted, "I respectfully withdraw my name and support my distinguished colleague, Estes Kefauver."

Kennedy watched as the delegates huddled and transferred votes. When the numbers were finally tallied, Kefauver had 775½ to Kennedy's 589.

Though Jack Kennedy was disappointed, he did achieve the national reputation he had been seeking. Adlai Stevenson summed up the experience: "As for Jack Kennedy, I have a feeling that we shall hear a great deal more from this promising young man."

Personal Sadness

A greater disappointment for Jack took place shortly after the convention. His wife, though eight months pregnant, had been with him throughout the grueling convention days. On their return to Massachusetts, Jack decided to fly to Europe with his brother, Ted, for a two-week yachting vacation in the Mediterranean. Jackie went to her family's home to rest.

On August 23, she was rushed to the hospital in Newport. The baby, a girl, was stillborn. When the news reached Jack three days later, he immediately flew home. Since this was the second baby that they had lost, it was a particularly hard time for both of them.

A Consolation Prize

When Jackie recovered, Kennedy did his best to help the party's candidates. He traveled to 26 states, campaigning even harder than the presidential and vice-presidential candidates. Though Eisenhower was returned to the White House, the Democrats held their majorities in both houses of Congress.

When the new Congress convened in 1957, Kennedy was rewarded for his efforts. For a long time, he had wanted to serve on the Senate Foreign Relations Committee. Estes Kefauver, who had served four years longer in the Senate, also wanted the assignment. But Kennedy's national popularity and his ability to get along with both young and older members of the Senate paid off. The Democratic steering committee, headed by Lyndon Johnson, awarded the plum appointment to Jack Kennedy.

Chapter 6
The Campaign Trail: Winning the Nomination

Shortly after the 1956 convention, a friend told Kennedy that he would have no trouble getting the vice-presidential nomination next time. Kennedy laughed, "Let's not talk about vice. I'm against vice in *any* form."

The 1956 Democratic convention, with its race for the vice-presidential nomination, had given John Kennedy national recognition and the assurance that he could make a successful run for the presidency. His re-election campaign for senator in 1958 reinforced his confidence. He not only got the largest total vote ever received by a candidate for any office in the state of Massachusetts, he won by a greater margin than any other candidate in the country who had run against opposition for a major office.

PLOTTING CAMPAIGN STRATEGY

On October 28, 1959, a group of 16 people met in the living room of Robert Kennedy's home in Hyannis Port. Their goal was to determine how the presidential campaign would be run. Among the group were six men who had already proven their ability to Kennedy and who would serve him with the utmost dedication through his presidency.

One of the men was Robert, now 33 years old, who had been and would continue to be Jack's campaign manager throughout the 1960 race. Others who were present included Kenneth O'Donnell and Lawrence O'Brien. O'Donnell was the tactician; he listened to and planned with Kennedy. O'Brien was the organizer; he took the game plan and made it work.

Also there was Ted Sorensen, who had been working beside Kennedy in his Senate office as well as on the campaign trail. Sorensen was, in Kennedy's words, "My intellectual blood bank." One of Sorensen's functions would be to review all major decisions on national or international issues.

Then there were Pierre Salinger and Louis Harris. Salinger, a former newspaperman and congressional investigator, was to serve as Kennedy's press secretary. Harris, at age 33, had earned a reputation as an analyst of public opinion. His company had aided Jack's 1958 senatorial campaign, and he would continue to help by polling people throughout the nation to determine the country's thinking and prejudices on a variety of issues.

At this meeting Kennedy provided a stunning performance of his ability to remember facts, names, and figures. Without any notes, he reviewed the political situation in each of the 48 states as well as in Alaska and Puerto Rico. The guests were awed by Kennedy's memory and his command of facts. One of them commented, "Jack can still drive down an avenue in Boston and remember which stores put up his campaign posters 10 years ago."

Psyching Out the Opposition

Kennedy's likely opponents at the Democratic National Convention would be Hubert Humphrey, Lyndon B. Johnson, and Adlai Stevenson. Senator Humphrey was not well known outside of his home state of Minnesota. Humphrey had to win popular support and build his name recognition by proving he could win in the primaries. The newspapers covered the important primaries and that meant much free publicity.

Senator Lyndon B. Johnson of Texas was the favorite of southern Democrats. Adlai Stevenson, despite his losses to Dwight Eisenhower in the presidential elections of 1952 and 1956, was still the hero of the liberals and the intellectuals. Though Stevenson would not campaign for the nomination, his supporters felt he would be the candidate if the convention were deadlocked—that is, if no candidate could get enough votes through the balloting.

Kennedy was the "new boy on the street." He had made enough speeches all around the country in the previous two years so that he had name recognition. During this period, while Kennedy was out making speeches, Humphrey had given his priority to staying in Washington and voting on important issues in the Senate.

Kennedy knew that he lacked the support of older politicians; he also faced blocs of votes already committed to other candidates. He needed to win such overwhelming popular support at the convention that even the professional politicians would be forced to support him on the first ballot. He had to prove his popularity by winning every one of the primary elections that he entered.

Sizing Up the Candidate

Aspects of the Kennedy personality and campaign were also discussed during the October 28 session in Hyannis Port and others that followed.

or leaving work, they seemed cold or indifferent. But day after day, he walked and talked with people when they gave him a chance, and he listened to their problems.

Even Jackie came to help. Though she was pregnant, she wanted to do her part. One time, in Kenosha, she entered a supermarket just as the manager was announcing the day's specials over the loudspeaker. With a warm smile, she asked permission to speak on the microphone. Shoppers were surprised to hear, "Just keep on shopping while I tell you about my husband, John F. Kennedy." Then, in her soft, charming manner, Jackie told them about his wartime service and his accomplishments in Congress. At the end she added, "He cares deeply about the welfare of his country—please vote for him."

Jack tried to downplay the religious issue. Nevertheless, the biggest paper in the state, the *Milwaukee Journal*, on the Sunday before the election, published an analysis dividing the voters into three columns—Republican, Democrat, Catholic. When the returns came in, friends celebrated that Kennedy had won 56 percent of the vote. But Jack was less than pleased when he realized that he had rolled up his biggest margin in Catholic districts and had lost in the Protestant districts.

Facing the Religious Issue

It was now clear that the religious issue had to be faced openly. West Virginia, which was 95 percent Protestant, was the next battleground.

On April 25, two weeks before the West Virginia primary, Kennedy decided to raise the religious issue. Silence on the subject seemed to feed the fears of those who had concerns about a Catholic in the White House. Although religion had always been considered a subject that political candidates should not and did not discuss, Kennedy said, "I

Psyching Out the Opposition

Kennedy's likely opponents at the Democratic National Convention would be Hubert Humphrey, Lyndon B. Johnson, and Adlai Stevenson. Senator Humphrey was not well known outside of his home state of Minnesota. Humphrey had to win popular support and build his name recognition by proving he could win in the primaries. The newspapers covered the important primaries and that meant much free publicity.

Senator Lyndon B. Johnson of Texas was the favorite of southern Democrats. Adlai Stevenson, despite his losses to Dwight Eisenhower in the presidential elections of 1952 and 1956, was still the hero of the liberals and the intellectuals. Though Stevenson would not campaign for the nomination, his supporters felt he would be the candidate if the convention were deadlocked—that is, if no candidate could get enough votes through the balloting.

Kennedy was the "new boy on the street." He had made enough speeches all around the country in the previous two years so that he had name recognition. During this period, while Kennedy was out making speeches, Humphrey had given his priority to staying in Washington and voting on important issues in the Senate.

Kennedy knew that he lacked the support of older politicians; he also faced blocs of votes already committed to other candidates. He needed to win such overwhelming popular support at the convention that even the professional politicians would be forced to support him on the first ballot. He had to prove his popularity by winning every one of the primary elections that he entered.

Sizing Up the Candidate

Aspects of the Kennedy personality and campaign were also discussed during the October 28 session in Hyannis Port and others that followed.

John Kennedy's youthful appearance was both an asset and a liability. For those looking for vitality, a new face on the national scene, and a fresh approach to politics, Kennedy was appealing. For those looking for maturity and the wisdom that should go with it, John Kennedy, at age 43, was just too boyish. After all, no President had ever been so young.

His access to money had its good and bad sides as well. With financial backing from his father and his father's business connections, Kennedy could afford not only a well-paid campaign staff and expensive publicity, he could even afford his own plane. Ted Sorensen, who traveled with Kennedy from 1956 on, remembers horrendous congressional campaign trips on small private planes, in snowstorms and fog, sometimes with inexperienced or amateur pilots. One time, during a torrential downpour, they took off from a bay in Alaska in a seaplane, the Senator working the windshield wiper by hand.

In 1959, the family purchased an airplane and named it *Caroline*, after Jack's daughter, who was born in 1957. The plane, complete with desk, kitchen, and bedroom, allowed the candidate to plan his own schedule and to arrive in a more rested condition. Other candidates were not so fortunate, and there were those who accused Joe Kennedy of buying the election for his son.

The press made much of John Kennedy's "charisma," his wit and charm, and his ability to make each individual he met feel important. It enabled him to gather a well-organized group of volunteers and professionals dedicated to his cause. Yet, beneath that charm, he could be, as one biographer who knew him well said, "hard, ruthless and unscrupulous."

Obstacles Ahead

The road to the White House had many roadblocks, however. One was that John Kennedy was a Catholic, and no Catholic had ever been elected President. In 1928, another Catholic, Alfred E. Smith, had tried but failed miserably.

Another issue was Jack's health. No matter how hard the family tried to keep secret the news about his physical condition, rumors abounded that he lived on drugs and was in poor health. In reality, however, his physical condition in 1960 was generally far better than it had been in prior years. The fact that he had the stamina to criss-cross the country, stand outdoors in all kinds of weather at welcoming receptions, and rush from one speaking engagement to another should have squelched all rumors about his health.

Kennedy's silence on McCarthyism also made many liberals afraid of supporting him. At the same time, southern Democrats felt his increasing interest in the civil rights issue made him "too liberal."

All these were part of the problems Kennedy knew he would have to deal with as he officially announced his candidacy for President on Saturday, January 2, 1960, at a jam-packed press conference.

ROUND ONE: THE PRIMARIES

The New Hampshire primary is always the nation's first. Hubert Humphrey did not file for it, however, because the state is a neighbor of Massachusetts, and Kennedy territory. The first meeting ground for the two candidates was Wisconsin—Humphrey territory, next to his home state. The entire family, with the exception of Joseph Kennedy, was recruited for the battle. (Joseph never appeared publicly during the campaign. Whatever he accomplished was done behind the scenes.)

Those first primary days were ones John Kennedy would never forget. Early one morning, his motorcade stopped at the N-Joy cafe, where he hoped to find a rally of supporters. Instead, he found only eight people. He spoke at high schools, hoping the students would tell their parents about him. When he stopped at factories to greet men and women coming to or leaving work, they seemed cold or indifferent. But day after day, he walked and talked with people when they gave him a chance, and he listened to their problems.

Even Jackie came to help. Though she was pregnant, she wanted to do her part. One time, in Kenosha, she entered a supermarket just as the manager was announcing the day's specials over the loudspeaker. With a warm smile, she asked permission to speak on the microphone. Shoppers were surprised to hear, "Just keep on shopping while I tell you about my husband, John F. Kennedy." Then, in her soft, charming manner, Jackie told them about his wartime service and his accomplishments in Congress. At the end she added, "He cares deeply about the welfare of his country—please vote for him."

Jack tried to downplay the religious issue. Nevertheless, the biggest paper in the state, the *Milwaukee Journal*, on the Sunday before the election, published an analysis dividing the voters into three columns—Republican, Democrat, Catholic. When the returns came in, friends celebrated that Kennedy had won 56 percent of the vote. But Jack was less than pleased when he realized that he had rolled up his biggest margin in Catholic districts and had lost in the Protestant districts.

Facing the Religious Issue

It was now clear that the religious issue had to be faced openly. West Virginia, which was 95 percent Protestant, was the next battleground.

On April 25, two weeks before the West Virginia primary, Kennedy decided to raise the religious issue. Silence on the subject seemed to feed the fears of those who had concerns about a Catholic in the White House. Although religion had always been considered a subject that political candidates should not and did not discuss, Kennedy said, "I might just as well discuss the issue that all the voters are thinking about."

In Morgantown, West Virginia, Jack suddenly left his prepared speech and said, "Nobody asked me if I was a Catholic when I joined the United States Navy." The crowd stared in disbelief. He went on, "Nobody asked my brother if he was Catholic or Protestant before he climbed into an American bomber plane to fly his last mission." A man in the audience blurted out, "Pretty good speaker, I'd say."

The reactions to Kennedy's remarks were so positive that he continued to raise the subject, not only in West Virginia but also at a meeting of the American Society of Newspaper Editors. "I am not the Catholic candidate for President. I do not speak for the Catholic Church on issues of public policy and no one in that church speaks for me. Are we to say that a Jew can be elected Mayor of Dublin, a Protestant can be named Foreign Minister of France, a Moslem can sit in the Israeli Parliament but a Catholic cannot be President of the United States?"

Two days before the West Virginians were to go to the polls, Kennedy went on television with the issue. With him was Franklin Roosevelt, son of the President most revered in West Virginia, Franklin Delano Roosevelt. Kennedy reminded them that in 1948 Catholic Boston had overwhelmingly voted for Baptist Harry Truman "because of the man he is. I would like the same fairness Harry Truman was shown."

The issue had become intolerance. The only way a West Virginian could prove he was *not* a bigot was to vote for Kennedy. And they did. On May 10, West Virginia endorsed the Kennedy candidacy by a 61-39 margin, upsetting the predictions of many of the leading newspapers. There were those who again complained that Joe Kennedy had "bought the election" for his son. The leading newspaper in the state, the

Charleston Gazette, sent out reporters to check the facts. The editor summarized the investigation: "Kennedy did not buy the election. He sold himself to the voters."

West Virginia had also sold itself to Kennedy. One of the outcomes of campaigning there was that John Kennedy gained an insight into a grinding poverty that he had never truly understood before. The visits to tiny villages in the poorest mining areas, a descent into a coal mine to see the laborious hard work, the hunger on the faces of women and children touched him as never before. His first-hand experiences enabled him to speak emotionally and with knowledge about the many needs he saw in the state.

On primary election night, Humphrey conceded not only the primary but his run for the presidential nomination. He was exhausted by his statewide travels in a lonesome bus with the sign, "Over the Hump with Humphrey." He was drained from the daily expenses he could not meet. The defeat left him without funds to carry on the campaign.

Jack Kennedy had already returned to Washington when Humphrey made his announcement. But Robert Kennedy sloshed through a miserable rain at one o'clock in the morning to go to personally thank Humphrey for his letter of congratulations. Humphrey offered graciously to meet John Kennedy when he returned to Charleston to claim victory. Robert Kennedy was touched by the offer, and arm in arm the two men walked back to Kennedy headquarters in the rain.

ROUND TWO: THE DEMOCRATIC CONVENTION

With Humphrey now on the sidelines, Kennedy might have taken time for a well-deserved rest. Instead, he spent the seven weeks before the national convention appearing before Democratic state committees and meeting with professional politicians and party leaders. He still had two formidable opponents, Lyndon Johnson and Adlai Stevenson, the undeclared candidate.

National events had given a boost to both of these candidates. A few days before the West Virginia primary, Francis Gary Powers, flying a high-altitude plane, called a U-2, over the Soviet Union, became the first American spy ever shot down and seized by the Russians. As a result, a meeting between President Eisenhower and the Soviet Premier, Nikita Khrushchev, collapsed shortly after it began in Paris. Disarmament negotiations between Russia and the United States broke down.

Adlai Stevenson had long been considered an expert in foreign affairs. Lyndon Johnson, as majority leader in the Senate, had earned a reputation as a master at guiding important issues through the Senate. Now the burning issue before the Senate dealt with foreign affairs. By comparison with these two mature and experienced men, Kennedy seemed to many to be a boy playing a grown man's game.

Truman and the Youth Issue

Shortly before the convention, former President Harry S. Truman delivered what could have been a knock-out blow to Kennedy's candidacy. In a televised address, Truman endorsed Johnson and several other candidates. He then proceeded to attack Kennedy on his age and experience.

"Senator, are you certain that you are quite ready for the country, or that the country is ready for you in the role of President . . . ? [We need] a man with the greatest possible maturity and experience . . . May I urge you to be patient?"

Once again, Kennedy made the most of the attack. In a televised press conference, he reviewed his 14 years' experience as a member of Congress. He then went on, "[If]

14 years in major elective office is insufficient evidence, that rules out all but a handful of American Presidents, and every President of the 20th century—including Wilson, Roosevelt and Truman."

Kennedy then added that if age, not experience is the test, then it would eliminate "from positions of trust and command all those below the age of 44, [and] would have kept Jefferson from writing the Declaration of Independence, Washington from commanding the Continental Army, Madison from fathering the Constitution . . . and Christopher Columbus from even discovering America."

Kennedy's words cleverly deflected the age issue, leaving his opponents with their own problems. Stevenson was a two-time loser and Johnson represented a minority, southern whites. To many in the North and Midwest, Johnson's drawl and his overly dramatic expressions and gestures made him appear as a country bumpkin—a "cornball"—rather than a dignified and serious candidate. And though his friends had opened campaign headquarters almost a year earlier, Johnson did not officially announce his candidacy until July 5th, five days before the convention began.

First Ballot Victory

The Kennedy team went to the convention assured that they had the votes necessary to win on the first ballot. But strange things can occur at national conventions. Although confident, John Kennedy was careful not to appear cocky.

Late in the afternoon on Wednesday, July 13, the nominating speeches began. Kennedy's was delivered by Governor Orville Freeman of Minnesota, a liberal, a Protestant, and a friend of the farmer. Among those who gave seconding speeches were a woman, a black, and a southern Governor-elect.

The Campaign Trail: Winning the Nomination 63

Though the speeches for Kennedy were received with excited demonstrations, they could not match the drama and intensity of Stevenson's nomination. When Senator Eugene McCarthy of Minnesota finished his eloquent speech, demonstrators poured in from all the gates, screaming and chanting, "We want Stevenson." From the galleries packed with supporters (but not delegates), banners were unfurled. Golden balloons floated down from the ceiling. The entire demonstration had been orchestrated by a former television producer. For a brief moment, even the Kennedy team, watching on television, began to show concern.

When the crowd would not respond to the pounding of the gavel of the chairman, Governor LeRoy Collins of Florida, he ordered the lights turned off, except for a single spotlight focused on the American flag. Stevenson's moment of glory faded with the lights. Despite the tremendous show put on by his supporters, when the final tally was completed, he had only 79½ votes.

When the roll call of states began at 10 o'clock that night, Kennedy sat watching it on a television set in a private apartment hideaway. To win the nomination, he needed 761 votes. According to the Kennedy strategists, if the roll call was over 700 by the time the state of Washington was polled, Kennedy would make it on the first ballot. Floor managers from the Kennedy team were alerted to watch closely as Washington was called.

After Washington was polled, the count read 710. West Virginia came through and made it 725, then Wisconsin added 23. The count was now 748. Wyoming had 15 votes. As John Kennedy watched, he saw his brother, Ted, moving among the Wyoming delegates. And then the Wyoming chairman announced, "Wyoming casts all 15 votes for the next President of the United States." John Kennedy was the presidential nominee of the Democratic Party!

In Search of a Vice-President

Current custom gives a party's presidential nominee the privilege of selecting his own Vice-President. Kennedy's selection surprised him almost as much as it surprised his supporters.

Before his nomination, Kennedy had mentioned to others that if *he* could not be President, Lyndon Baines Johnson was probably the most qualified man. But during the final days before the convention, harsh words had been exchanged between the two candidates. So Kennedy was more than a bit surprised when, after his nomination, he received a telegram that read, "LBJ now means Let's Back Jack."

For both men, the decision to offer or to accept the vice-presidential nomination was difficult. Yet, when Kennedy called Johnson the next day, they agreed to meet that morning at 10:15. At that session, Johnson told Kennedy that he was available. They parted, each to discuss the idea with party leaders.

Two weeks before the convention, Ted Sorensen had assured Kennedy that making such an offer would be a smart move. "After all, he is the leader of the party in the Senate, is already a national figure, and is the leader who has the most strength in that part of the country opposed to you."

Big city liberals and labor, however, were vehemently opposed to Johnson, in part because of his stand on labor issues. Moreover both Bob Kennedy and Ken O'Donnell had assured these groups that Kennedy would never select Johnson.

Some of Johnson's advisors urged him to refuse—that he was needed in the Senate and that being the majority leader was more important than being Vice-President. Others told him to take it—that his strong following in the South and West would make a winning ticket. Several friends reminded him that being Vice-President would enhance his national reputation. Lady Bird Johnson, Lyndon's wife, suggested that after his recent heart attack, the job of Vice-President might be less strenuous than the Senate job.

For Kennedy, it took some serious and smooth talking to convince labor and the angry liberals. But they finally had to concede that a Kennedy-Johnson ticket had the best chance of winning.

On the closing day of the convention, Adlai Stevenson, in a move to create party harmony, introduced the nominee. Kennedy seemed exhausted. The arena was only half filled and at first the audience did not seem very responsive. But as Kennedy drew toward the end of his acceptance speech, his voice gathered strength. In ringing tones he concluded, "Now begins another long journey, taking me into your cities and homes all over America. Give me your help, give me your hand, your voice and your vote!" The crowd rose to its feet and cheered. The Kennedy-Johnson ticket was on its way!

Chapter 7
The Youngest President

John F. Kennedy's road to the Democratic nomination took almost nine long months, with the candidate fighting every step of the way. On the other hand, Richard Nixon's nomination as the Republican candidate for President was an accepted conclusion long before the Republicans met in Chicago. He was already the Vice-President of the United States; he had a national and international reputation; he had experience with the Soviet leader, Nikita Khrushchev; and he had the endorsement of President Eisenhower.

On Wednesday, July 27, Nixon was unanimously voted the 1960 standard bearer for the Republican Party. His choice for Vice-President was Henry Cabot Lodge—the man Kennedy had defeated for the Senate eight years earlier. Lodge was a good choice, for Nixon had declared as his campaign strategy, "If you ever let [the Democrats] campaign only on domestic issues, they'll beat us—our only hope is to keep it on foreign policy." In addition to having been a U.S. senator, Lodge had also been the representative of the United States to the United Nations.

TELEVISION DEBATES AND OTHER SPEECHES

Kennedy had no objection to debating foreign policy. In the months between the West Virginia primary and the convention, Fidel Castro, the Cuban leader, had seized all private American property in Cuba and had openly allied himself with the Soviets. That, plus a sudden downturn in the economy, provided more than enough issues for a unique event: a series of four Kennedy-Nixon televised debates that were held in September and October.

The debates themselves did not clarify the issues. However, the power of television to project personality was proven decisively. The image created by Kennedy's calm command of the situation and his knowledge of the facts was clearly projected by the television screen. As a result, he won support from some who had been less than enthusiastic about him—in particular, a group of 10 southern governors.

The basic difference between the two contenders during the campaign seemed to be attitudes more than issues. Nixon talked in glowing and positive terms about America's strength, leadership, and economic success. Kennedy pointed to problems such as unemployment, pollution, defense, and education. He talked about a "New Frontier," of "uncharted areas of science and space, unsolved problems of peace and war, unconquered pockets of ignorance and prejudice, unanswered questions of poverty and surplus." Kennedy described the difference in the campaign as a contest "between the comfortable and the concerned."

Nixon insisted on bringing up Kennedy's background. "It's not Jack's money he's spending, it's yours. He may have more money, but you have more sense." Despite the fact that he did not like Nixon—the man or his style—Kennedy refrained from making personal attacks.

The Power of Television in Politics

In 1953 there were 27 million television sets in the United States. Seven years later, by the 1960 presidential conventions, there were 76 million sets, and some politicians began to realize that television could be more than just a medium for entertainment. John F. Kennedy was one of those who recognized that television and politics were made for each other.

Other political figures had already used television successfully. In 1952, when he was accused of improperly accepting money from some campaign contributors, Vice-President Richard Nixon decided to make a television appearance to clear his name. By talking about his wife's "Republican cloth coat" and his dog, Checkers, Nixon diverted attention from the issue of questionable contributions. President Dwight Eisenhower was the first President to televise his press conferences to keep the American public informed. But it was the Kennedy personality combined with television that changed American politics dramatically.

The 1952 presidential campaign was the first real demonstration of the power of television on political events. For the first time, the American people could see, as well as hear, the candidates' speeches. At the conventions, they could absorb the carnival atmosphere—the bands, the bunting, the music, the mobs of delegates and reporters. They could even get a peek into committee debates.

Television created new patterns of behavior. It brought political personalities into the family living room. It expanded the audience of the nominating conventions from 12,000 people sitting in a convention hall to 100 million Americans sitting at home in front of their television screens. With such a mass audience, convention schedules were streamlined and both parties tried to time important speeches for prime viewing time.

John Kennedy got his first major national prime-time coverage when he lost the nomination for Vice-President at the 1956 Democratic convention in Chicago. When he realized that he had lost to Estes Kefauver on the third ballot, he rushed from his hotel to the convention hall. Walking up to the platform, he began to speak. His words were brief and touching. As 100 million Americans watched, Kennedy said, "I hope you'll make [Kefauver's nomination] unanimous." The convention crowd roared its approval. The audience at home saw the image of a gallant and gracious loser, and they were captivated. Television had turned a loser into a winner.

The 1950s also marked a decline in the power of political parties as television and public relations gained in importance. Television appearances and commercials could reach more people than were ever reached in town meetings and by trains or planes. Kennedy's relaxed manner, his boyish good looks, and his humor were perfect for this new means of communication.

If any proof was needed, about the power of television, the Nixon-Kennedy debates in the 1960 presidential campaign proved the point. Both men were well prepared, and both spoke well. But television accentuates facial characteristics. Nixon's deep-set eyes and heavy brows cast a shadow on his face. Moreover, because he has a dark beard, an advisor applied a pancake make-up to his face; that made him sweat. Nixon also wore a white shirt that reflected the glare of the lights. And because he had recently lost weight, his shirt seemed to gape at the neck.

Kennedy, on the other hand, was suntanned and wore a blue shirt that did not reflect the glare of the lights. He looked crisp and calm while Nixon looked hollow-eyed, pale, and nervous.

Up until that time, the largest television audience had been for the final game of the 1959 World Series, when 90 million Americans watched the Los Angeles Dodgers beat the Chicago White Sox. The total audience for the Nixon-Kennedy debates exceeded that figure. Though most commentators felt both men had been good debaters, the television audience overwhelmingly favored Kennedy. As one columnist, Ralph McGill, said, "Maybe the TV audience looked more than it listened." No doubt about it. In sample polls of those who *heard* the debate on radio, Nixon and Kennedy received equal ratings; those who *saw* the debate rated Nixon's performance as "poor." As

> Kennedy stated after the election results were in, "It was TV more than anything else that turned the tide."
>
> As television gained in importance as a campaign medium, tremendous sums of money were spent for air time. The Republican Party spent $500,000 on television the Monday before the 1960 election. Today, more and more of a candidate's campaign money is poured into television time. Almost all candidates hire public relations firms to "polish their image," for they know that how a candidate looks and projects to an audience may be more important than what he says.
>
> Many serious people are asking questions about the power of television. Does television favor politicians who can present the best dramatic performance? Does it favor the candidate who can buy the most time? Is the personality of a candidate becoming more important than the issues? These are good questions that may in the future require serious consideration.

Kennedy's speeches lasted no longer than 20 minutes for major occasions and only five minutes for daytime stops. They often were sparked by humor, some planned, some ad libbed for the occasion. At one stop, he noted that much of the yelling and jumping came from a group of children. "If we can lower the voting age to nine," he joked, "we are going to sweep this state."

When members of a Young Republicans group interrupted him by chanting, "We want Nixon," Kennedy smiled and called out, "I don't think you're going to get him," and the crowd cheered.

ON THE CAMPAIGN TRAIL

A great part of the success of Kennedy's campaign was due to the work of his "advance men" and his attitude toward the press. Advance men arrive in a town or city several days before the candidate. Working with local party leaders, they plan every detail of the candidate's visit, from the route of the motorcade to the distribution of flags and buttons, from hotel accommodations for the candidate and his aides to hotel arrangements, food, and transportation for the members of the press. When Kennedy arrived, an advance man would brief him with important names and faces, a schedule, and information about the local community. On the campaign trail, the careful scheduling of every moment of Kennedy's valuable time depended on the work of the advance men.

Traveling with the candidate were 40 to 50 experienced reporters, representing the nation's biggest newspapers. Nixon had the support of about 75 percent of the newspaper publishers in the country, but he did not trust reporters. They, in turn, found him hard to approach—aloof and standoffish. While reporters covering Nixon occasionally were invited aboard the candidate's plane, there were always three representatives of the press, on a rotating basis, aboard the *Caroline*. The friendliness, the humor, and the warmth in the Kennedy camp probably influenced reporters to write in a manner sympathetic to his candidacy. By the end of the campaign, these reporters became Kennedy's friends. Many had become devoted admirers.

Scheduling Strategy

To win the presidency, a candidate had to have 269 electoral votes. Nine states held 237 electoral votes among them. Seven of the nine states were clustered in the Northeast, and it was there that Kennedy concentrated his efforts. Lyndon Johnson was assigned the eighth state, Texas, and Kennedy spent four days in California (the ninth state), leaving the balance of the campaign in that state to Stevenson. In all, Kennedy visited 45 of the 50 states. (Both Alaska and Hawaii had achieved statehood in 1959.) To keep to his schedule, Kennedy had to speak eight to 10 times a day, sometimes in as many as five states. In one week, he criss-crossed the country to speak in 27 states.

The days were grueling and seemingly endless. Dave Powers, Jack's old friend from Boston, often found it hard to waken Kennedy in the morning. One of Dave's favorite tricks was to arouse Jack with, "What do you suppose Nixon's doing while you're lying there?" Yet, once out on the campaign, Jack seemed to get renewed energy from the enthusiasm of the crowds.

A big factor in Kennedy's success was the effort to register large numbers of new voters. As a result, seven million new voters were added to the roles, three-quarters of whom registered as Democrats.

Another factor was Kennedy's immediate response to the plight of the black civil rights leader, Dr. Martin Luther King, Jr. On October 24, Dr. King was one of 51 people arrested in Atlanta, Georgia, protesting segregation at a restaurant. All the prisoners were released except for King, who was sentenced to four months in a rural prison on the charge that his driver's license was no longer valid in Georgia. When a member of his staff notified Kennedy of the incident, he immediately telephoned King's pregnant wife. Robert Kennedy followed up with a call to the judge on the case and Dr. King was released.

Blacks had not been particularly sympathetic to Kennedy. Many felt that he had not given adequate support to the civil rights cause; others were concerned about his religion. But his compassionate response to Dr. King's situation immediately raised his popularity among black voters.

The Longest Day

The last week of the campaign showed Nixon and Kennedy seesawing back and forth in the polls. The election turned out to be a "cliff-hanger," with the results hard to predict.

Election day, November 7, was a bright, sunny day as Mr. and Mrs. John F. Kennedy voted in Boston in the Sixth Ward. Then they flew back to Hyannis Port to await the results. It was, as Jackie described it, "the longest day." News trickled in slowly, and the mood changed from elation to worry and back again as trends began to develop. Through it all, the candidate kept his sense of humor. At one point, Lyndon Johnson called from Texas. Kennedy laughed as he reported LBJ's comment: "I see *we* won in Pennsylvania, but what happened to *you* in Ohio?"

By three o'clock in the morning, the electoral votes stood at 261 for Kennedy, as they had for several hours. At four o'clock, Kennedy went to bed.

Meanwhile, in Washington, the head of the Secret Service, Urbanus E. Baughman, also waited. Sixteen agents had been sent to each candidate's headquarters, ready to protect the President-elect. At 5:45 in the morning, Baughman watched as Michigan's 20 votes were entered on the television screen, making the electoral vote 285 — over the top for Kennedy! Immediately, Baughman called his agents in Hyannis Port. Within an hour, maximum security had been established at the Kennedy compound.

At 9:30 A.M., Ted Sorensen arrived and was immediately identified by the Secret Service. He was the first to tell John Kennedy that he had been elected. It was after 1:00 P.M. when the whole Kennedy family proceeded to the local armory to meet with haggard reporters who had been waiting all through the long night. As Kennedy stood up to read the congratulatory telegrams from Nixon and President Eisenhower, some said there were tears in his eyes. Seated in the front row was his father, Joseph Kennedy.

That afternoon, expressions of horror flickered across the faces of the Secret Service men as the President-elect quarterbacked a ferocious game of touch football with his family on the spacious lawn. A typical Kennedy celebration!

72 DAYS TO GO

"If I am elected, I don't want to wake up on the morning of November 9th and have to ask myself, 'What in the world do I do now?' "

Shortly after his nomination, Kennedy called Clark Clifford, a former Special Counsel to President Harry Truman. Confidently looking ahead to a victorious election, Kennedy wanted to be as well prepared on Inauguration Day as he was for the Democratic convention. He invited Clifford to develop plans for the new government.

Kennedy was quite concerned about the fact that he had won by such a small margin. True, the electoral vote was 303 to 219, but Kennedy received 49.7 percent of the popular vote against Nixon's 49.6 percent. If only two people in each district had voted differently, Nixon would have been the winner.

Because he wanted to get his administration off to a good start, Kennedy sought out a group of bright people with a variety of viewpoints. "I can't afford to have only one set of advisors," he said to Richard Neustadt, a college professor from Columbia University, whose suggestions he also requested. Kennedy wanted to see all his options, all the problems, and then make his own decisions.

On November 9 Clifford appeared with a thick handbook that would be a guide to the many tasks to be completed by Inauguration Day. As the 72 days drew to a close, most of the work had been done. The new Cabinet had been formed, and most of the other 1,200 appointed positions had been filled. Kennedy had asked for the best and he got them, Democrats and Republicans. He seemed to be staffing a university rather than a government of politicians.

In early December, President Eisenhower and Kennedy met formally for the first time. Kennedy studied very carefully for the meeting. The 75-minute session changed the outgoing President's opinion of Kennedy, whom he had previously called a "young whippersnapper." Eisenhower's aides later leaked out the information that the President was "overwhelmed by Senator Kennedy, his understanding of world problems, the depth of his questions, his grasp of the issues, and the keenness of his mind." Eisenhower's new esteem for Kennedy helped the transition from the old administration to the new.

Thanksgiving was a quiet family dinner in the President-elect's home in Georgetown, a section of Washington. Late that evening, he boarded the *Caroline* to go to Palm Beach for a working session with his staff at the family home. His plane, now on its way to Florida, received word that Jackie was on the way to the hospital. Their new baby was about to arrive, two weeks early. Once again, John Kennedy was not there. He immediately took a plane back to Washington, where Jackie and his new son, John F. Kennedy, Jr., awaited him.

Chapter 8
The White House, Kennedy Style

Fire and ice. Film stars and poets. The old and the young. The inauguration, on January 20, 1961, of John Fitzgerald Kennedy included all these elements.

Snow began falling the evening before the inauguration. By the time Jacqueline and John Kennedy started to visit all the inaugural festivities, eight inches of snow blanketed the city. However, the snow did not seem to deter the crowds who had come to see the President-elect and the other celebrities attending the ceremony.

By the next morning the snow had stopped, and the sun struggled to make an appearance. But a biting wind and a 20-degree temperature promised a frigid Inauguration Day. At Kennedy's request, the new Cabinet members and White House officers were dressed in formal clothes — including top hats — a sign of the kind of dignity and style Kennedy wished to bring to the presidency.

The great American poet, Robert Frost, began to read a poem he had written for the occasion, but the glare of the sun and the snow made it so difficult to read that he decided to recite an older poem from memory. And when Richard Cardinal Cushing of Boston began to deliver a prayer for the

Inauguration Day, January 20, 1961. Coatless and hatless, John F. Kennedy became the 35th President of the United States and the youngest man to ever enter the White House. The new Vice-President, Lyndon Johnson, stands behind Kennedy. Jacqueline Kennedy, the new First Lady, is at the far left. (John F. Kennedy Library.)

new President, smoke began to rise from a short circuit in the microphone's electrical system. Firemen and Secret Servicemen worked frantically, worried that they might have to stop the proceedings and evacuate everyone from the grandstand. Fortunately, the problem was solved quickly.

As Kennedy rose to take the oath of office, one could not help but contrast the old and new leaders. At age 70, Dwight Eisenhower was, at that time, the oldest President to serve in that office. At age 43, John F. Kennedy was the youngest. One sentence in his inaugural speech illustrated this contrast: "Let the word go forth from this time and place, to friend and foe alike, that the torch has been passed to a new generation of Americans."

Before beginning his inaugural address, Kennedy removed his topcoat and placed his top hat, which he had been carrying, on a chair. Now bareheaded and coatless, his very presence gave an air of youth and vigor.

The closing words of his inaugural address became a theme for his administration:

> And so, my fellow Americans, ask not what your country can do for you; ask what you can do for your country.
>
> My fellow citizens of the world, ask not what America will do for you, but what together we can do for the freedom of man.
>
> Finally, whether you are citizens of America or citizens of the world, ask of us here the same high standards of strength and sacrifice which we ask of you. With a good conscience our only sure reward, with history the final judge of our deeds, let us go forth to lead the land we love, asking His blessing and His help, but knowing that here on earth God's work must truly be our own.

NOW IT'S REAL

John Kennedy was thoroughly delighted by living in the White House. Though he had spent years pursuing his dream, the first few days there seemed unreal. On his second day as President, he decided to show his brother, Ted, his new place of work, the Oval Office. With them was Paul Fay, an old buddy from PT boat days and newly appointed under secretary of the Navy. Spinning around in his swivel chair, Kennedy asked what they thought about the place. Paul Fay's comment summed up all their feelings: "I feel any minute somebody's going to walk in and say, 'All right, you three guys, out of here.'"

As President, Kennedy wanted to be informed and efficient. He also wanted to balance his day so that he had time to relax and unwind with his family and friends. His schedule was never exactly the same, but a sample day might have looked somewhat like this:

A Day in the Life of the President

7:30 – Kennedy awakens and begins reading the morning papers. This is followed by a series of phone calls he makes to get further information or suggest action on something he has read. (During the course of the day, that might mean as many as 50 calls.)

8:30 – After a bath, he has breakfast with his wife and children (or a breakfast meeting with staff members or leaders of the Senate or House of Representatives).

9:00-9:30 – Walks to office, sometimes with Caroline tagging along. Checks the mail and reads a six- to eight-page memo from the Central Intelligence Agency (CIA). Begins series of meetings. These might include conferences with:
- a foreign ambassador paying a formal call at the beginning or end of his stay in Washington
- members of the Cabinet
- members of Congress, to talk over a piece of legislation
- White House aides, to discuss an upcoming press conference

During these sessions, much of the time was spent by Kennedy in gathering data on problems and political situations, both in this country and abroad. He once commented, "The more people I can see, or the wider I can expose [my mind] to different ideas, the more effective [I] can be as President."

He always managed to find time to read the weekly reports from each of the government departments. One official who had served through many administrations

The White House, Kennedy Style 83

President Kennedy at his desk in the Oval Office of the White House, the place where he worked and met with his staff, congressmen, and foreign dignitaries. (John F. Kennedy Library.)

noted, "I never heard of a President who wanted to know so much."

1:00 – A 15-minute swim in the White House pool, in water heated to 90 degrees, with his old friend and aide, Dave Powers. This is followed by special exercises to strengthen his ailing back.

1:30 – Lunch with business or labor leaders, or with foreign officials or newspaper editors, followed by a nap in his bedroom.

3:30 – Back to the office for more conferences, or to read or sign documents or prepare for a press conference.

7:30–8:30 – Depending on how much work he has to finish, the President has dinner with his wife and friends, often following up with a movie in the special White House viewing room. If he found the film boring, he might leave and return to his office for a few more hours of work.

The President summed up his feelings about being a resident in the White House in 15 words, "I have a nice home, the office is close by, and the pay is good." Actually, Kennedy always donated his government salaries as representative, senator, and President to a variety of charities.

The White House Children

One advantage of living in the White House was that it gave John Kennedy a chance to really know his children. When his daughter, Caroline, had been born, Kennedy had been so busy running for the presidency that he barely had time to get to know her. Now he could be a real father to Caroline and her new brother, John, Jr. Both children were lively and bright, and into as much mischief as "any kid in town." Caroline would clatter into a staff meeting, teetering on a pair of her mother's high-heel shoes, or wander into the press lobby and blithely inform the reporters that her father was "sitting upstairs with his shoes and socks off not doing anything."

It was hard to keep the two children out of the public eye, and the press loved to report on their activities. Caroline was 3½ years old and John, Jr., only two months old when the family settled into the White House. During the presidential years, the children met more heads of foreign governments than most politicians. They charmed everyone with their good manners and funny comments, and for their father, they were a source of constant joy and delight.

Jacqueline and John Kennedy with their children, Caroline and John. Caroline is astride her pony, "Macaroni." (John F. Kennedy Library.)

Jacqueline Kennedy and the Cultural Revival

As First Lady, Jacqueline Kennedy was once asked what she viewed as her role in the White House. She replied, "I think the major role of the First Lady is to take care of the President . . . [and] if you bungle raising your children, I don't think whatever else you do well matters very much."

In her years as First Lady, the White House became both an elegant mansion and a showplace for the talented men and women of the nation in the sciences and the arts, including theater, dance, music, and film. The President once joked at a White House dinner in honor of André Malraux, the

Jacqueline Kennedy was one of the youngest and most beautiful women to be a First Lady. Her work in the historic restoration of the White House remains as part of the Kennedy legacy. (John F. Kennedy Library.)

French Minister of Culture, "I am very glad to welcome here some of our most distinguished artists. This is becoming a sort of eating place for artists. But they never ask *us* out." Under Jacqueline Kennedy's guidance, the White House was redecorated to preserve the mansion's history and beauty for future generations. She appointed a commission to assist her in accurately recreating historical periods with furniture, paintings, and fixtures. She raised money for the restoration by creating the White House Historical Association, which publishes a guidebook and other pamphlets about the mansion, its history, and the people who have lived there.

In February 1962, Mrs. Kennedy, a very private person, finally agreed to host a television tour of the newly restored White House. Though television critics could not resist making fun of her quiet, whispery voice, the show achieved what she had wanted. The number of people who toured the public rooms of the White House from 1960 to 1962 increased more than 60 percent.

Until his marriage, Kennedy had little interest in the arts. It was Jacqueline who changed the description of state dinners from staid and stuffy to elegant, cultured, and amusing. The stage was set by the exquisite food, prepared by a French chef, the fine wine, the beautiful flowers, and the strolling musicians provided by the Air Force. The First Lady, in a French designer gown, and the President, in white tie and tails, greeted their guests with warmth, a personal comment, and often a touch of humor.

Following dinner, there would be entertainment in the East Room. Here guests would listen to such great musicians as violinist Isaac Stern or cellist Pablo Casals, or watch the performance of a Shakespeare theater company.

Perhaps the most exciting of these dinners was one held, not for the visit of a foreign head of state, but for American Nobel Prize winners. No President had ever officially honored these brilliant scientists. Smiling at his guests that night, Kennedy proclaimed, "This is the most extraordinary collection of talent . . . that has ever been gathered together at the White House—with the possible exception of when Thomas Jefferson dined alone."

President Kennedy was a man who sought and appreciated excellence in any endeavor. He recognized the talents of the artists and scholars and the importance of their contribution to American culture. By their efforts to display and honor these men and women, John and Jacqueline Kennedy created in Americans a new popular interest in their arts and sciences.

Sadness Strikes Twice

Just as in any home, life at the White House has its darker moments. On Thanksgiving Day, 1961, Joseph Kennedy suffered a stroke. Despite the efforts of the best doctors, he became permanently crippled and unable to speak. Communication between father and son, which had been so important to both of them, suffered most of all. The President tried to repay the years of his father's devotion and love by visiting with him often, both in Palm Beach and in Hyannis Port, even taking him sailing when the weather permitted.

The personal event that probably affected Kennedy most was the death of his infant son, Patrick, in August 1963. The baby was born with a lung ailment. All the country waited for news about the infant as he was moved from one hospital to another and placed in a special high-pressure oxygen chamber. The President kept vigil at the hospital, but at four in the morning, the boy's heart failed. The President uttered not a word—just left the room so no one would see his tears. Throughout the nation, people grieved with Mrs. Kennedy and the President.

Chapter 9
The Heights and the Depths

The first few months of a new presidency tend to be a "honeymoon" period. The people and the Congress generally allow the new administration to get its people in place and its programs started. Both the nation and the Congress tend to be accepting of new ideas. Certainly the Kennedy administration was on a "high." Everything seemed to be going according to plan.

Congress and the people seemed satisfied with the high quality of the Kennedy team. Traditional Democrats were pleased to see Adlai Stevenson named Ambassador to the United Nations. The Republicans were pleased to see two of their own as cabinet members. The politicians even accepted Bobby as Attorney General despite his youth and inexperience.

The idea of a New Frontier, as expressed in Kennedy's campaign speeches, captured the imagination of America. A new spirit of vigor and change seemed to be coming from Washington. Kennedy's first executive order doubled the amount of surplus food for four million hungry Americans, thereby keeping his promise to the people of West Virginia. He communicated with the public through live television press conferences, and the people seemed to enjoy Kennedy's relaxed and natural manner with reporters. The polls gave him a growing rate of approval.

SOME EARLY UPS—AND DOWNS

Nothing symbolized the spirit of the New Frontier more than the President's order, in March 1961, creating the Peace Corps. The Corps was designed to bring the skills and talents of young (and older) Americans to poor countries, to help the people there help themselves. Peace Corps members worked at such diverse tasks as digging wells, demonstrating new farming methods, teaching, nursing, and developing native crafts into money-making industries. It also was hoped that Peace Corps members, by their efforts, would promote friendship between the countries in which they worked and the United States.

The program was so successful that by 1964 there were 10,000 volunteers working in 46 countries. The American ambassador to Venezuela commented, "It has worked miracles in changing the Venezuelan image of North Americans. Before the Peace Corps, the only Americans the poor Venezuelans ever saw were riding around in Cadillacs. They supposed them all to be rich and selfish. The Peace Corps has shown them an entirely different kind of American."

A Cuban Failure

The mood did not last long. As someone described the events of April 17–19, 1961, "While Kennedy was still trying to move in the furniture, . . . he found the roof falling in and the door blowing off." The disaster, called the "Bay of Pigs," was based on a plan developed during the Eisenhower administration.

At Kennedy's last meeting with Eisenhower, on the day before the inauguration, they discussed the situation in Cuba. Eisenhower urged the President-elect to follow through on a plan for overthrowing the Communist government of Fidel Castro. A military force, called the Cuban Brigade, had begun training in Guatemala in March 1960. It started as a guerilla group that intended to infiltrate Cuba and win support of local populations for the overthrow of Castro. It was to be a covert (secret) operation, conducted by the Central Intelligence Agency (CIA).

During the months following Kennedy's last meeting with Eisenhower, a new plan for Cuba was devised. Now it was to be a military invasion; air strikes from Nicaragua would destroy Castro's air force and be followed by a landing of 1,400 men at the Bay of Pigs on the southern coast of Cuba.

Kennedy listened to the CIA explanations, the comments of the Joint Chiefs of Staff, and the State Department. The President finally agreed to the plan but without use of American armed forces in Cuba. It was to be a Cuban-sponsored and Cuban-fought operation.

As it turned out, the operation proved to be too big to be secret, too small to be successful. The invading Cubans fought valiantly for three days against more than 20,000 of Castro's soldiers. In the end, the survivors were captured and sent to prison.

The plan had been poorly designed and badly organized. The Cuban Brigade lacked adequate ammunition and air cover. Information about Castro's popularity and the loyalty of his soldiers was inaccurate. Kennedy's reputation around the world slipped, and articles were published blaming him for pushing Castro into the arms of the Soviet Union.

It was the most serious mistake of Kennedy's career, but he profited from the experience. He had accepted the advice of "experts" whose ability he did not know personally, and he had not adequately used people whose background and intelligence he trusted. He was determined that this incident would not be a permanent blot on his administration. Most important, he wasted neither time nor energy blaming others. He publicly took responsibility for the disaster . . . and moved on.

The Race In Space

In 1957, the Soviets were the first to launch a satellite into space. Though the exploit jolted the American public, the Eisenhower administration failed to put much effort or funding into an American space program. Then, in April 1961, the Soviets flew the first manned orbital space flight. Although Alan B. Shepard, Jr., became America's first man in space the following month, it was not until February of 1962 that the first American, John H. Glenn, Jr., orbited the earth.

In Kennedy's second State of the Union message to Congress in May 1961, he pledged to land a man on the moon and return him safely to earth within 10 years. The idea was exactly the spark Congress needed. That year the space budget was increased by 50 percent. The thrust that the Kennedy government gave the space program enabled astronauts Neil Armstrong and Edwin Aldrin, Jr., to walk on the moon in July 1969.

The Foreign Issues

Many of the world's leaders were both curious and concerned about the new American President—in many instances, a man young enough to be their son. Particularly interested was the Soviet leader, Nikita Khrushchev, whose major concern in the spring of 1961 was West Berlin.

Following World War II, a defeated Germany was divided into West Germany (German Federal Republic) and East Germany (German Democratic Republic). The city of Berlin also was split: East Berlin was occupied by the Russians; West Berlin was occupied by the western powers (France, England, and the United States). Unfortunately, the city of Berlin was located, like an island, in the East German zone. The continued presence of western allied troops and the prosperous, capitalist economy in West Berlin was a thorn in the side of the Soviet Union and its puppet government in East Germany.

After the Bay of Pigs fiasco, Khrushchev was convinced that Kennedy was a weak leader, that if pushed hard, he would back down rather than stand firm and risk war. Khrushchev felt the time was ripe to press for a formal treaty recognizing the German Democratic Republic and making Berlin a unified "free city." That formula would have given East Germany control of all the travel routes in and out of Berlin. It would have meant the withdrawal of western allied troops, seriously damaging the morale of West Germans now allied with the United States, France, and England. It would have been viewed as a sign of weakness throughout the world.

A meeting between Kennedy and Khrushchev was planned without definite negotiations in mind. Rather, it was to be an opportunity for the two leaders to size each other up and to exchange ideas. So, for three days in June of 1961 at Vienna, Austria, the two men, working through interpreters, debated Communism versus Capitalism, the independence of Laos, nuclear test ban agreements — and Berlin.

Kennedy found Khrushchev to be a tough opponent, who argued, challenged, and would not give an inch. The experience shook the young President. He had gone to Vienna as an innocent beginner working with world leaders. He had faced a shrewd, cunning, and unpredictable enemy. Kennedy was exhausted by the experience, but he now knew what kind of man Khrushchev was and how his mind worked. He would be ready when the next round came.

"Oui, Oui, Jackie!"

Not all the leaders Kennedy met on that trip abroad were as difficult. On the first stop, which was in Paris, France, he found he had an ally who was able to turn the proud and very nationalistic French leader, Charles de Gaulle, from a lion to a pussy cat. That ally was Jacqueline Bouvier Kennedy. Her French heritage made the Parisiens feel she was one of them. When Jackie appeared for a magnificent French dinner at the Versailles Palace in an exquisite white lace gown, with her hair piled high in 14th-century fashion, even the French reporters declared her *"Charmante! Ravissante!"* ("Charming! Ravishing!").

The crowds followed her wherever she went, and De Gaulle was enchanted by her perfect French and her knowledge of French history. Her conquest of De Gaulle and the French people was so complete that at a press luncheon, Kennedy introduced himself as "the man who accompanied Jacqueline Kennedy to Paris."

In their meetings, De Gaulle urged Kennedy to stay neutral in Southeast Asia. He observed that the land was not good for traditional kinds of warfare fought by western troops. De Gaulle also told Kennedy that it was important to impress on Khrushchev that the western powers would not retreat from West Berlin (which Kennedy did his best to convey later at the Vienna meeting). It was also reassuring to hear similar words about Berlin when he met Prime Minister Harold Macmillan of England on the last lap of his trip.

A Warning About Vietnam

Macmillan and Kennedy had met earlier, at which time Macmillan had warned Kennedy against involvement in Southeast Asia. England was concerned that continued assistance to Laos would pull America into a war. He urged Kennedy to try for political negotiations rather than military action. But Eisenhower had already committed "advisors" (troops who trained the local people) to the area. Kennedy had followed with two Marine divisions, and the Seventh Fleet was now there. To back down now would look like "appeasement," giving in to the growing Communist threat in the region.

By the end of 1962, 10 times more Americans were killed or wounded in South Vietnam than in 1961. The foundation was laid for the full-blown Vietnam War, which would erupt in 1962 and wrack the United States for the next 11 years.

Chapter 10
Standing Firm

The Vienna meeting left President Kennedy deeply concerned about Soviet intentions. There was little doubt that Khrushchev was going to apply pressure. But where was he going to push first—Southeast Asia, Berlin, or Cuba? The answer came quickly.

The President's plane, *Air Force One*, had hardly touched down at Andrews Field, outside of Washington, on its return from Vienna, when Kennedy learned that Khrushchev had ordered an increase of three billion rubles in the Russian military budget. Kennedy's response was to double the call for American draftees, and to increase the American military budget by $3 billion. The words and actions of the two most powerful men in the world shook the international scene—and particularly the people of Berlin.

During July 1961, more than 30,000 people fled from East to West Berlin. Then, during the first 10 days of August, another 16,500 fled into the western sector. Among the refugees were skilled workers and technicians, the cream of East German talent needed for its industrial development. In desperation, Walter Ulbricht, the Communist leader of East Germany, decided to act. Shortly after midnight on August 13, 1961, a convoy of tanks and trucks rumbled into the dark, deserted streets of East Berlin. By sunrise, the beginnings of a wall were already in place—a wall of barbed wire and stone blocks that, when completed four days later, was a prison for the Germans of East Berlin.

FACING UP TO THE BERLIN WALL

Though the building of the wall was a tragedy for East Germany, it did not basically change the allies' position. They were still in West Berlin, and the people living there still had the freedom to choose their own form of government. The only question was whether they would still have access to West Germany through East Germany.

Kennedy decided to test Soviet intentions. He ordered a convoy of 1,500 American soldiers to ride in armored trucks over the highway from West Germany, through the East German checkpoints, to West Berlin. In order to keep up the spirits of the West Berliners, Kennedy dispatched Vice-President Lyndon Johnson to the besieged city. There he promised American support of West Berlin with "our lives, our fortunes, our sacred honor."

One day, at the height of the crisis, Andrei Gromyko, the Soviet ambassador to the United States, arrived at the White House bearing a letter from Nikita Khrushchev — and a small, white, fluffy puppy, a gift for Mrs. Kennedy. At a dinner party, during the Vienna meeting, Jackie had commented to Khrushchev that she would like a puppy from the first dog sent into space by the Russians. John Kennedy stared at the puppy and then at his wife. Jackie covered her mouth and whispered, "I was only trying to make conversation."

The Khrushchev letter was warm and friendly, and it was followed by more letters and visits from Ambassador Gromyko, with suggestions for making West Berlin an international zone. Kennedy turned him down. It was now clear that Khrushchev was not about to go to war over Berlin. The Berlin crisis was over — a stalemate. The wall remained, but the road to West Berlin was open, and there was no war.

"Ich bin ein Berliner"

Kennedy became a hero to the people of West Berlin. When he visited there in June 1963, the Berliners gave him one of the greatest receptions of his life. Three-fifths of the city's population turned out to welcome him.

After visiting the Berlin Wall, President Kennedy spoke from a platform outside the city hall. As he spoke, applause and cheers followed his words. He concluded: "All free men, wherever they may live, are citizens of Berlin, and, therefore, as a free man, I take pride in the words, *'Ich bin ein Berliner.'* " ("I am a Berliner.")

A tumultuous roar of approval echoed through the square. Later that day, Kennedy, exhausted, sat quietly recalling the day's events with Ted Sorensen. "We'll never have another day like this one as long as we live."

STEEL BENDS TO AN IRON WILL

The year 1962 gave President Kennedy ample opportunity to prove he could be a firm and resolute leader. For some time, he had been concerned about inflation. One of the basic industries, steel, was an important component of the price index. By holding down the price of steel, the cost of other products—automobiles, machinery, refrigerators, and other appliances—could be kept low.

Early that year, Secretary of Labor Arthur Goldberg began helping the steel industry negotiate a reasonable pay increase for its workers. The contract, signed in April by both the workers and management, was "the least costly agreement in many years." Goldberg, in meeting with the chairman of the largest steel company, United States Steel, declared that the amount of the increase was so small that the steel companies would not have to raise their prices.

On April 10, on the same day that the last major contract was signed, the U.S. Steel chairman came into Kennedy's office. He handed the President a printed sheet announcing a $6 a ton increase in the cost of steel, four times the cost of the wage increase. The President, in a steely voice, said, "I think you're making a mistake." Secretary Goldberg and the union were not so kind. They called it a "double-cross."

Quickly and quietly, Kennedy began working behind the scenes. He asked the Attorney General, his brother, Robert, whether such a price increase by all the steel companies was a violation of laws against monopolies. The President ordered the Bureau of Labor Statistics to show that the steel industry needed no increase, and how the increase would harm the nation's economy and damage the defense budget. And at the next morning's press conference, he told the whole story to the American public. Members of the Kennedy staff also quietly called upon three smaller steel companies that had not yet agreed to the price increase and asked their chairmen to hold the price line. They agreed.

Within 72 hours, Kennedy was able to announce that the $6 increase announced by U.S. Steel was being dropped. The steel industry had surrendered to the President's iron will.

CIVIL RIGHTS NOW!

Though John Kennedy had supported the pressure for more racial equality during his years in Congress, he had not pushed hard for tough civil rights legislation as President. He believed that black civil rights would come without a revolution. More important, he knew he did not have the votes in Congress to get such legislation passed. The country needed to be educated, and the time was not yet ripe.

What Kennedy had not counted on was the growing desperation of the blacks and the powerful impact of such men as Dr. Martin Luther King, Jr. How could the country, in September 1962, be celebrating the centennial of the Emancipation Proclamation, the document that led to the freeing of the black slaves, when the blacks were still discriminated against in employment, housing, voting, and education? The blacks who began mounting a campaign for civil rights in 1961 thought that they would get support from the White House, but so far, little had come.

Their confidence in Kennedy was tested in May 1961, when a group of black and white "Freedom Riders," dedicated to doing away with discrimination on public transportation, began a series of trips through Alabama on public buses. When the buses were burned and the riders beaten by mobs, Kennedy was forced to take action. He sent 600 deputy federal marshals to Montgomery to protect the riders.

Under Attorney General Robert Kennedy, the Department of Justice began a series of lawsuits against segregation in airports and railroad stations. It took time, but soon all travel terminals were available to blacks and whites on equal terms.

At the Schoolhouse

The next major test came in September 1962. James Meredith, a black with nine years of service in the Air Force, applied for admission to the University of Mississippi. He arrived at the school, accompanied by federal marshals, only to be denied entry by the governor of Mississippi, Ross Barnett. Both the President and the Attorney General called Barnett personally. When they could not get assurance that Meredith would be registered without harm, the President federalized the Mississippi National Guard and ordered United States Army troops to the area.

Federal marshals accompanied Meredith to the campus again, while Deputy Attorney General Nicholas Katzenbach and federal officials waited in a college building called the Lyceum. A crowd gathered outside. As the day lengthened, the mob, now 2,500 strong, began to toss bottles and bricks. The federal marshals were forced to use tear gas and the mob, now growing with out-of-state groups, began using shotguns and rifles.

Katzenbach called for help. The President ordered the National Guard and the Army to the scene. By the time the troops quelled the riot, two men had been killed and hundreds wounded. Meredith was admitted, under the protection of federal marshals, and graduated in August 1963.

The Flame Burns in Alabama

Fanned by the violence in Mississippi, the flame of equality flared up in Birmingham, Alabama, in April and May of 1963, when Dr. Martin Luther King, Jr., led sit-ins to desegregate restaurants and other public places. The American public saw on television the local police commissioner order the police to attack unarmed blacks and whites with clubs, police dogs, and fire hoses. Kennedy ordered 3,000 troops to the area and the violence subsided.

When the governor of Alabama, George Wallace, attempted to stop two black students from enrolling at the University of Alabama, Kennedy was ready. Katzenbach was on the scene with the National Guard. Wallace backed down and the last state university in the country was desegregated.

The people had witnessed the violence of the spring of 1963 on television. The American public recognized that action on civil rights had to be taken. On June 19, President Kennedy sent to Congress the most complete civil rights legislation ever proposed.

"I Have a Dream"

It was a glorious day. The hot, strong sunlight sparkled on the white stones of the Washington Monument and the Lincoln Memorial. Massed on the mall between the two monuments were 250,000 people—black and white, young and old—representing virtually every religion. They had come to Washington by train, plane, bus, automobile, bicycle, and some even by foot. Among the crowd were movie stars. There was a winner of the Nobel peace prize, Dr. Ralph Bunche, and baseball's first black star, Jackie Robinson.

They were there to make known to Congress and to the millions of people watching on television that the time for racial equality in the United States was "Now!" President Kennedy's civil rights bill had to be passed at the coming session of Congress. Blacks were no longer willing to wait. Too much had happened that year.

That spring and summer, Americans had watched racial violence in Jackson, Mississippi, in Birmingham, Alabama, and in Greensboro, North Carolina. On June 11, after the President spoke that night on television about the moral crisis in the nation, Medgar Evers, a black civil rights leader, had been murdered in front of his home in Jackson, Mississippi.

Now, on that August day, the President sat in the White House, watching the events on television. He had worried that such a large gathering of people might get out of hand, but the crowd was orderly, peaceful, well-mannered. The leaders of the march had promised the President that trained marshals would help maintain order. They had kept their word.

One of the best-known black leaders, A. Philip Randolph, expressed it best. "We are not a pressure group, not an organization or a group of organizations. We are not a mob. We are the advance guard of a massive moral revolution for jobs and freedom."

Then Dr. Martin Luther King, Jr., the last speaker, walked quietly to the microphone. The crowd was hushed and intent as he said, "I have a dream." He concluded his speech with, "When we let freedom ring, when we let it ring from every village and every hamlet, from every state and every city, we will be able to speed up that day when all God's children, black and white men, Jews and Gentiles, Protestants and Catholics, will be able to join in the words of that old Negro spiritual, 'Free at last! Free at last! Thank God almighty, we are free at last!'"

With King's last words still echoing through the air, the crowd quietly dispersed. The leaders of the march joined President Kennedy at the White House. He greeted them with the words, "You did a superb job in making your case." When he discovered they had not eaten since breakfast, he ordered food for them. For everyone, the day had been a remarkable and memorable occasion.

> The 1963 March on Washington was one of the most moving and dramatic events of the Kennedy era. It made Americans aware that not only blacks, but whites of all religious persuasions were behind the civil rights movement. It provided President Kennedy with the strong demonstration of public support that he needed in order to get his civil rights bill passed.

TO THE BRINK

Today, in the offices or homes of 15 men who served in the Kennedy administration sit prized mementos of one of the most critical periods in U.S. history. It is a small silver calendar of October 1962, with 13 days, October 16 through 28, deeply engraved. It was a gift from President Kennedy for the participation of these men in one of the most awesome decisions any President ever had to make. It began at 8:00 A.M. on October 16 with a visit from White House aide McGeorge Bundy.

Tuesday, October 16

"Mr. President," says Bundy solemnly, "there is now photographic evidence that the Russians have offensive missiles in Cuba."

The news does not shock the President. The alliance between Cuba and the Soviet Union has existed for some time. In August, because of intelligence reports, the President has ordered increased use of aerial reconnaisance planes to photograph Cuba and every ship bound for it.

But why had Russia decided to place bases capable of launching intermediate-range ballistic missiles within range of United States territory? Was it to make the United States look weak in the eyes of the world if we took no direct action? And if the United States did attack "little Cuba" as a response, would it divide the allies and cause Latin America to become more anti-American?

By 11:45 that morning, a group of men assembles as a special committee. Among them are Secretary of State Dean Rusk, Secretary of Defense Robert McNamara, Attorney General Robert Kennedy, and Secretary of the Treasury Douglas Dillon. They will be joined later by CIA Director John McCone.

At that first meeting, all are pledged to secrecy and to maintain a normal routine as much as possible so that the press and Russian intelligence will not be aware that these special meetings are being held. The President does not want to force a Soviet move or to panic the American people.

The task of the committee is to look at all the alternatives plus all the possible consequences of each action. The meetings will go on each day until a decision is made. This is not going to be another Bay of Pigs. This time, the President has a team of men whose judgment and experience he knows and trusts.

Thursday, October 18

The committee is informed by United States intelligence that the Cuban missiles will be capable of killing 80 million Americans within a few minutes after their launch.

Some members of the team push for an invasion of Cuba. Others suggest an air strike to destroy the missile bases before they can be completed. Time is running out. Daily aerial photographs show that work on the Cuban bases is moving rapidly. It is McNamara who suggests a naval blockade. A legal advisor from the State Department, aware that a blockade is considered an act of war, suggests using the term "quarantine" instead.

Saturday, October 20

The President, finishing a speaking engagement in Chicago, receives a call from Robert Kennedy. "The final decision has to be made now," Robert tells his brother. As the President departs for Washington, Pierre Salinger, Kennedy's press secretary, tells the reporters that the trip has been cut short because the President has a cold.

On returning to the White House, Kennedy seeks out his wife and children first. He asks Jackie if she prefers to leave Washington with the children or stay in the White House, evacuating to a special underground shelter in case of air attack. Jackie tells him that she will stay with him and share whatever happens.

Sunday, October 21

Following a meeting with military leaders, Kennedy decides that a quarantine is to take place. He also decides to speak to the nation on Monday evening at 7:00 P.M.

Monday, October 22

American armed forces are put on worldwide alert and 180 naval vessels are sent to the Caribbean. Congressional leaders are flown by Air Force jet fighters to attend a 5:00 P.M. meeting with the President. Though there is some disagreement and tension, the President holds firmly to his decision. At 7:00 P.M., tuned to radios or seated silently before television sets all over the nation, the people listen intently to the President's words. He explains the secret deployment of the missile bases in Cuba, the danger to the United States, and the need to have them removed. He describes the quarantine as a means to prevent further buildup of Soviet military equipment in Cuba.

Tuesday, October 23

Messages from world leaders and the American people pour into the White House supporting Kennedy's action.

Wednesday, October 24

A convoy of Russian ships bound for Cuba is reported to have stopped, presumably to await orders from Moscow.

Friday, October 26

The Soviet ships have turned around and are on their way back to Russia. A letter is received from Khrushchev stating that the Soviet Union will withdraw the missiles if the United States will agree not to invade Cuba.

Saturday, October 27

Kennedy wires a response to Khrushchev, agreeing not to invade Cuba and to withdraw the quarantine provided the missile sites are removed.

Sunday, October 28

At 9:00 A.M. a bulletin from Moscow is broadcast to the American people at the same time that Kennedy receives a message from Khrushchev. The missiles will be withdrawn. The crisis is over.

Good Times

Only a week after the Cuban missile crisis was resolved, the Kennedys had another reason to cheer. The youngest brother, Edward "Ted" Kennedy, won Jack's former Senate seat. He beat Henry Cabot Lodge's son, George. With his three surviving sons now in top positions in Washington, father Joe's dreams have now been realized.

Chapter 11
"Promises to Keep"

On November 22, 1963, at 12:30 P.M. in Dallas, Texas, John Fitzgerald Kennedy was killed by an assassin's bullet. Cut down at age 46, the plans, aspirations, and dreams of the 35th President of the United States came to an abrupt end. What might have been had Kennedy survived to serve a second term in office?

The summer of 1963 had seen so many promising events, starting with the civil rights legislation the President sent to Congress on June 19. That same month, he had a memorable 10-day visit with world leaders in Berlin, Italy, and Ireland. He also stopped in England to pay the only visit he ever made to the gravesite of his beloved sister, Kick.

On July 25, the Soviet Union and the United States signed a Nuclear Test Ban Treaty. Within two months, it was passed by the Senate, becoming the first treaty to ban atomic explosions in the atmosphere, space, and under water. Communication between Kennedy and Khrushchev had improved so much that, by the end of the summer, a "hot line," a teletype link, connected the Kremlin in Moscow with the White House in Washington.

Kennedy had been looking forward to the trip through Texas in late November. It would mark the beginning of his 1964 campaign for re-election, and Jackie would be with him. He was feeling confident about the upcoming election and was sure that this time he would win with a big margin. Once

107

November 1963. The Kennedy family watches as the flag-draped casket of President Kennedy passes by. (John F. Kennedy Library.)

The burial place of President John F. Kennedy in Arlington National Cemetery. (John F. Kennedy Library.)

returned to office, he would no longer be distracted by the re-election process. (As a senator, he had voted for a two-term limitation on the presidency.) With popular support, he could push hard for the new legislation he would be proposing on the problems of poverty, unemployment, and mass transportation.

There were still grave international issues that needed attention. He wanted an undersecretary of state dedicated to the problems of Latin America. He was concerned that such conditions as poverty and illiteracy could create a climate for the expansion of Communism into Central and South America.

The assassination of South Vietnam President Ngo Dinh Diem on November 1 added to the instability in Southeast Asia. Kennedy was worried about the continuing buildup of

The John Fitzgerald Kennedy Library in Boston, Massachusetts. (John F. Kennedy Library.)

American troops in that area. There were only 200 Americans in South Vietnam when he had taken office; now, there were 16,000.

John Kennedy had always looked to the future. He had made plans for his presidency even before he was elected. He was planning now for all he wished to accomplish in the next five years. During his 1,000 days in office, he had given the American presidency a new style, one that prized intellect and reason. With the help of his wife, he had brought to the White House a new appreciation for the arts and American culture. He had gained the affection of the people of Europe as no President since Franklin Roosevelt.

John Kennedy loved being President. Ted Sorensen's eight-year-old son once sent him a letter in which he wrote that he would like to live in the White House some day. Kennedy scribbled back, "So do I . . . Sorry, Eric, you'll have to wait your turn."

It was a beautiful autumn day at the end of that October. President Kennedy flew to Amherst College in Massachusetts to speak at a ceremony to honor Robert Frost, the poet who had spoken at his inauguration. In his address, Kennedy spoke of his vision of America's future—a vision he did not live to see.

He had, instead, in the words of his favorite Frost poem, . . . "promises to keep, and miles to go before I sleep."

Bibliography

Burns, James MacGregor. *John Kennedy: A Political Profile.* New York: Harcourt Brace, 1960. This book, which was written as Kennedy was running for the presidency, gives a fairly easy-to-read background on the candidate's years leading up to the election.

Collier, Peter, and Horowitz, David. *The Kennedys: An American Drama.* New York: Summit Books, 1984. An interesting book for background on the Kennedy clan, from its arrival in the United States through the presidential years.

Donovan, Robert. *PT 109: John F. Kennedy in World War II.* New York: McGraw-Hill, 1961. In narrative style, this book details the experience that made John Kennedy a war hero.

Goodwin, Doris Kearns. *The Fitzgeralds and the Kennedys: An American Saga.* New York: Simon and Schuster, 1987. The author shows the parallel paths of the lives of these two prominent Irish families from immigrant days on. It provides more background on the family than on the career of its most prominent member, John F. Kennedy.

Levine, I. E. *Young Man in the White House: John Fitzgerald Kennedy.* New York: Julian Messner, 1964. This book deals more with Kennedy's personal life than his political life at a level students will enjoy.

Manchester, William. *One Brief Shining Moment—Remembering Kennedy.* Little, Brown, 1983. This book is easy reading and has many charming anecdotes about Kennedy's life, beginning with his days as a congressman.

O'Donnell, Kenneth, and Powers, David F., with Joe McCarthy. *Johnny, We Hardly Knew Ye.* Boston: Little, Brown, 1972. This book was written by two of the men who worked closely with Kennedy during his political career. They reveal the witty, sensitive, and more personal side of John Kennedy.

Parmet, Herbert S. *Jack: The Struggles of John F. Kennedy.* New York: Dial Press, 1980. This is the first in a two-volume series on the life of Kennedy. It describes the pre-presidential years with many insights into his personality.

Parmet, Herbert S. *JFK: The Presidency of John Fitzgerald Kennedy.* New York: Dial Press, 1983. The second volume of Parmet's work on Kennedy describes his years in the White House. It has good background and explanations of such events as the Cuban missile crisis and the civil rights movement.

Salinger, Pierre. *With Kennedy.* Garden City, NY: Doubleday, 1966. From the campaign days in September 1959 through the years of Kennedy's presidency, Salinger served as his press secretary. His knowledge of the workings of the press corps makes fascinating reading for anyone who has ever wanted to be a television or newspaper reporter—or just wants to know more about how news is gathered and reported.

Schlesinger, Arthur, Jr. *A Thousand Days: John F. Kennedy in the White House.* Boston: Houghton Mifflin, 1965. This is a personal memoir by one who served in the White House during the Kennedy years. It deals largely with foreign affairs since Schlesinger was a special assistant to the President in this area.

Sorensen, Theodore C. *Kennedy.* New York: Harper & Row, 1965. Outside of the family, Sorensen probably knew Kennedy professionally better than anyone else. Beginning in 1953, when Kennedy was a young senator, Sorensen became his speechwriter, researcher, and a man against whom Kennedy could play ideas and plans. The book is well indexed.

White, Theodore H. *The Making of the President.* New York: Atheneum, 1961. This large volume describes the 1960 campaign for the presidency. White writes as a reporter on the scene who traveled not only with the Kennedy press corps but, from time to time, with other candidates as well.

Index

Aldrin, Edwin, Jr., 92
Armstrong, Neil, 92

Barnett, Ross, 99
Bartlett, Charles and Martha, 44
Bay of Pigs, Cuba, 90, 91, 93, 104
Berlin Wall, 95-97
Berlin, West Germany, 92-97, 107
Billings, LeMoyne, 22, 23, 25, 32

Central Intelligence Agency (CIA), 82, 91
Chamberlain, Neville, 26, 28
Civil rights, 98-103
Clifford, Clark, 76, 77
Collins, Governor Leroy, 63
Communism, 36-38, 41, 47, 48, 109
Cuba, 90, 91, 95, 103-106
Cuban missile crisis, 103-106
Curley, James Michael, 31, 34-36

De Gaulle, President Charles, 93, 94
Democratic National Convention,
  of 1956, 50-52
  of 1960, 60-65
Dillon, Douglas, 104

Eisenhower, President Dwight D., 44, 50, 52, 61, 67, 69, 77, 80, 90-92, 94
Elizabeth II, Queen, 45
England (Great Britain), 37, 93
Evers, Medgar, 101

Fay, Paul, 81
Fitzgerald, John Francis (grandfather of John F. Kennedy), 14-17, 31, 34, 35, 41
Fitzgerald, Rose, see Kennedy, Rose
Fitzgerald, Thomas (great-grandfather of John F. Kennedy), 13, 14
France, 37, 93
Freedom Riders, 99
Freeman, Governor Orville, 62
Frost, Robert, 79, 111

Glenn, John H., Jr., 92
Goldberg, Arthur, 97
Gromyko, Andrei, 96
Gore, Senator Albert, 51

Harris, Louis, 54
Hitler, Adolph, 25, 26
Humphrey, Senator Hubert, 55, 57, 60

Ireland, 13, 107
  Great Famine of, 13

Johnson, Lady Bird, 65
Johnson, Lyndon B., 45, 52, 61, 62, 64, 65, 74, 75, 96

Katzenbach, Nicholas, 100
Kefauver, Senator Estes, 51, 70
Kennedy, Caroline (daughter of John F. Kennedy), 56, 84, 85
Kennedy, Edward (brother of John F. Kennedy), 19, 52, 106

117

Kennedy, Jacqueline Bouvier (wife of John F. Kennedy), 44–46, 52, 58, 75, 77, 85–88, 93, 94, 96, 105
Kennedy, John F.,
  as author, 26, 48
  campaign of, for President, 25–32
  campaign of, for Vice-President, 23
  campaigns of, for U.S. House of Representatives and Senate, 15, 16, 38–41
  health of, 17, 18, 24, 34, 37, 39, 47, 57
  and issue of Catholicism, 13, 14, 50, 51, 56, 58, 59
  marriage of, 43–45
  presidential inauguration of, 79–81
  as U.S. congressman, 34–38
  as U.S. senator, 45–49
Kennedy, John F., Jr. (son of John F. Kennedy), 77, 84, 85
Kennedy, Joseph (father of John F. Kennedy), 2, 15–26, 28–31, 41, 47, 48, 50, 56, 57, 76, 88, 106
  isolationism of, 26, 38
Kennedy, Joseph, Jr. (brother of John F. Kennedy), 19, 21, 22, 24, 27, 29, 30, 37
Kennedy, Kathleen (sister of John F. Kennedy), 23, 24, 26, 27, 29, 30, 37
Kennedy, Patricia (sister of John F. Kennedy), 33
Kennedy, Patrick (great-grandfather of John F. Kennedy), 13, 14
Kennedy, Patrick (grandfather of John F. Kennedy), 14–17
Kennedy, Robert (brother of John F. Kennedy), 19, 30, 32, 44, 49, 54, 60, 64, 74, 89, 99, 104
Kennedy, Rose (mother of John F. Kennedy), 19, 20, 33
King, Dr. Martin Luther, Jr., 74, 75, 99, 100, 103

Korean War, 39
Khrushchev, Nikita, 61, 67, 92–96, 107

Latin America, 109
Lodge, Henry Cabot, Jr., 38, 39, 41, 67
Lodge, Senator Henry Cabot, Sr., 41

Macmillan, Prime Minister Harold, 94
McCarthy, Senator Eugene, 67
McCarthyism, 39, 47, 48, 50, 57
McCormack, John W., 34, 35
McNamara, Robert, 104
Manchester, William, 34
Marshall, George C., 36
  Marshall Plan, 36, 37
Meredith, James, 99, 100

Neustadt, Richard, 76
New Frontier, 68, 69
Nixon, Richard M., 49, 67–69, 71, 74, 75
Nixon-Kennedy debates, 68, 71
Nuclear Test Ban Treaty, 107

O'Brien, Lawrence, 54
O'Donnell, Kenneth, 54, 64

PT 109, 1–7
Peace Corps, 90
Powers, Dave, 32, 74, 83

Randolph, Philip, 102
Roosevelt, Eleanor, 50
Roosevelt, President Franklin D., 25, 28, 29, 47, 59
Rusk, Dean, 104
Russia, *see* Soviet Union

Sallinger, Pierre, 54, 105
Shepard, Alan B., Jr., 92
Smith, Alfred E., 56

Sorensen, Theodore C., 49, 51, 55, 56, 65, 76, 97, 111
Southeast Asia, 93, 94
Soviet Union (Russia), 92, 93, 95, 96, 103–106
Space program, 92
Steel industry, 97, 98
Stevenson, Adlai, 50, 51, 61, 63, 65, 74, 89

Television, 41, 51, 61, 68–72, 87, 89

Truman, President Harry S., 36, 59, 61, 62, 76

United Nations, 29

Vietnam War, 44, 49, 111

West Germany (German Federal Republic), 92, 93, 95–97
Wallace, Governor George, 100
World War II, 27–29